A W

THE DOCTORS OF DOWNLANDS

Further Titles by Claire Rayner from Severn House

COTTAGE HOSPITAL
THE DOCTORS OF DOWNLANDS
THE FINAL YEAR

THE DOCTORS OF DOWNLANDS

Claire Rayner

This revised edition, complete with new introduction,
first published in Great Britain 1994 by
SEVERN HOUSE PUBLISHERS LTD of
9–15 High Street, Sutton, Surrey SM1 1DF.
Originally published 1968 in paperback format only by
Transworld Publishers Ltd under the pseudonym of Sheila Brandon.
First published in the U.S.A. 1994 by
SEVERN HOUSE PUBLISHERS INC., of
475 Fifth Avenue, New York, NY 10017.

British Library Cataloguing in Publication Data
Rayner, Claire
  Doctors of Downlands
  I. Title
  823.914 [F]

  ISBN 0-7278-4577-2

Typeset by Hewer Text Composition Services, Edinburgh.
Printed and bound in Great Britain by
Redwood Books, Trowbridge, Wiltshire.

INTRODUCTION
By Claire Rayner

Twenty-five or more years ago, I was a young would-be writer, trying to learn how to make my way in the world of books. I was writing for magazines and newspapers and I'd produced a couple of non-fiction books, but story-telling . . . that was a mystery to me. I knew I liked stories, of course; I've been an avid reader since before I was four years old and to this day I'm a pushover for a well-told tale. But how to tell a tale – *that* was the mystery.

So much so that it simply did not occur to me that I might be able to write fiction. But I was persuaded to try my hand. And because I knew that it is a basic rule of the learner writer always to write what you know, I opted to write about hospital life. After twelve years of sweat, starch, tears and bedpans as a nurse and then a sister in a series of London hospitals, I had an intimate knowledge of how such establishments work. I also knew that a great many people love peering behind closed doors into worlds they don't usually get the chance to experience.

So, I had a go. I started to tell myself stories of hospital life – rather romantic, but none the worse for that – only instead of keeping them in my own head as I had when I'd been a day-dreaming youngster, I struggled to put them on paper. And to my surprise and delight I found that publishers were willing to have a go, and gamble on me. They put my words into books – and I was delighted.

But also a bit embarrassed. I know it isn't an attractive trait to admit to, but there it is – I was a bit of a snob in those days. Not a social snob, you understand, but an intellectual snob. I had the notion that stories like these were a bit 'ordinary', that what really mattered was Literature with a capital 'L' and I knew perfectly well I wasn't writing that! So instead of using my own name on my first published attempts at story-telling, I borrowed my sister's first name and a surname from elsewhere in my family. And Sheila Brandon was born.

Now I am no longer a literary snob. I know that any storytelling that gives pleasure and interest to readers is nothing to be ashamed of and has a right to exist. It may not be Literature, but then what is? Dickens was just a story-teller in his own time, the equivalent of the writers of 'Eastenders' and 'Coronation Street'. Today he is revered as a Classic. Well, these stories of mine are never going to be classics, but I don't think, now I re-read them, that I need blush too much for them. So, here they are, the first efforts of my young writing years, under my own name at last. I hope you enjoy them. Let me know, either way!

CHAPTER ONE

It was all I could do to hear my own voice above the noise of the trains shunting past the nearby platforms, the porters' shouts, the rattle of mail trolleys, and all the rest of the hubbub of a main London terminus, let alone hear David's. Which was just as well, really. The whole thing was so miserable and difficult that having to shout at each other made it somehow easier to control the way we were feeling. And I didn't have to be told in so many words how David was feeling – I knew. I knew because I felt the same way.

It had all happened so quickly. There we had been, jogging along happily, David at University but living at home with Dad, me blissfully happy at the Royal as a paediatric house physician, seeing a lot of Charles –

And then, the whole word had come tumbling round my ears. The coronary attacks that had snuffed out Dad's life so suddenly and so cruelly had forced me out of my happy job, forced me to find another one where I could earn more, enough not only to keep myself but to keep young David at University to finish his training.

"But I've *got* to," I'd explained to Charles, when he'd told me brusquely that I was being absurd to sacrifice my career for a young brother who probably wouldn't appreciate it anyway. "My father did it for me, Charles

1

– he worked eighty hours a week, fifty-two weeks a year, running his workshop and looking after us after my mother died. He put me through University, and always swore he'd do the same for David. Well, he started the job, and – and I've got to finish it for him."

I'd swallowed hard and managed not to cry, because Charles hated weeping women.

"You must see that, Charles. And David *will* appreciate it, I know he will. Oh, he's a bit wild, I know that – but most boys of eighteen are a bit wild – I daresay you were." Charles had shaken his head irritably, but I'd persisted.

"Anyway, there it is. Maybe – maybe, later on, once David's through his course and can earn his own living I'll be able to – to come back. Back to paediatrics, I mean."

And I'd blushed absurdly. Why not admit to him that I was as miserable at leaving him behind in London as at leaving my absorbing job? But I couldn't, not to Charles, remote and handsome Charles who made me feel so very odd whenever I caught sight of his tall figure striding through the hospital corridors.

But that was something I'd never see again, I thought bleakly, as I leaned out of the train window and tried to hear what David was shouting. And I'd have to get used to the idea somehow –

"– only a fiver, Flip," David bawled, looking up at me appealingly, and I sighed, and began to riffle through my handbag.

"I can't do this often, David," I shouted back. "I'll be sending your board and lodging money to your landlady every week, and I'll send you some spending money whenever I can, but you'll have to manage somehow on your grant – "

David crinkled his eyes at me in that familiar wicked

2

way of his, and miserable though I was, I had to grin back at him.

"I mean it," I said, trying to sound severe. "We're on our own now, feller. Dad – Dad isn't there to see you through the way he used to, and I won't have that much to play with – not as a country GP – "

But I said the last words so quietly he couldn't hear them, for I didn't want him to. It wasn't David's fault I had to take a dreary job in a dreary town miles from the London I loved, buried in the backwaters of medicine. Dad had made a doctor of me, and I'd promised him, in that terrifying time between his first and second heart attacks, during that brief half hour when he knew he was dying and tried to tell me what to do, I'd promised him that David *would* be a lawyer, promised him I'd see the boy through. So that was that.

There was a new and even noisier bustle at the far end of the train, and a shudder ran through it. I leaned out of the window in a madly precarious fashion, and hugged David hard.

"Take care of yourself, feller," I said, and I couldn't help letting the tears drip down my nose. "Call me if you need me, you hear? But Heaven help you if you act the fool and get yourself into trouble – I'll murder you."

And I managed to smile through my tears, and stayed leaning out of the window watching his slight figure dwindle and finally disappear as the train curled away from the platform, gathering speed as it slid past the sooty old houses and dingy factories, the soaring new blocks of flats and tangled ribbons of railway lines, heading for the middle of England.

The trouble with train journeys is that they give you too much time to think. I sat curled up in the corner of the

3

compartment, glad I had it to myself so that I could repair the ravages to my make-up that my tears had made, trying to read the *Lancet* and the *British Medical Journal*.

But it was no good. I let the heavy journals slide off my lap and stared out at the wintry fields and woods, chilly under the thin morning sunshine of early spring, hardly seeing them.

Tetherdown. What sort of place would it be? I hadn't been able to find out. No one I knew had ever heard of the place, let alone been there. Somewhere between Fenbridge and Droitwich, that was all I knew, serving as the market centre for a farming area, but with a small industrial estate on the outskirts that was bringing new prosperity to a sleepy town. That was what Dr Redmond had told me when he had come up to London to interview me for the job as assistant to the practice.

"It's a rare treat for me to come up to town, my dear," he'd said to me over lunch at the Royal. "And an even rarer one to come back here to my own old hospital."

He'd sighed sharply and added: "It's just as well, I suppose. Let an old codger like me loose here, and I'd make a sorry fool of myself, wouldn't I? I make a good country doctor – I'd really be a fool if I didn't know that – but here with all these high-powered people – well!" And he'd looked across the dining-room to the table where the senior consultants sat in their lordly seclusion and for a moment looked sad.

"I'd hoped, once, you know, I'd hoped – pathology, that was my fancy. But it wasn't meant, so I'm just a country GP – "

He'd looked at me then, and laughed and patted my hand, and said: "And very glad to be one, and looking forward to having you join us in the practice.

4

It's worthwhile work you know, very worthwhile, and immensely interesting. So don't think you'll be bored, now, because you won't, I promise you – "

But his reassurance cut no ice at all with me. General practice was a dead loss, I could see that. The backwater of a career, a waste of ambition. And because of the cruel, heartbreaking accident of a coronary attacking poor Dad's over-worked heart, that was the backwater where I was to be washed up, where I was to flounder my frustrated ambition away. And a wave of resentment washed over me, making me feel sick with dull anger.

It's not fair, I thought childishly. I was going to be Dr Phillipa Fenwick, the paediatrician to whom the profession would look for guidance on all aspects of child health. I was going to be the best damned specialist in the diseases of children there could be. And now what? Dr Phillipa Fenwick, dreary dingy country GP. That was what –

But then I shook myself, and said aloud: "Stop it, idiot." It *was* idiotic to moan like this, to feel sorry for myself. It couldn't be helped, and anyway – and now a wave of optimism came up and sent the resentment away – anyway, it was only for a little while. Three more years, and David would have qualified, be ready to make his own way without my help. And I'd still be only twenty-seven then – still have time to get back on to the road I'd planned for myself.

But what about Charles? a secret voice whispered. Where does he fit into all this? Will he still be there three years from now, still be waiting for you?

I let myself think about Charles, painful though it was. He was such an *exciting* man, so very much what any young woman would dream about. Already a consultant physician, although he was only thirty-three, devastatingly

5

good-looking with his prematurely grey hair that made him look so distinguished, his tall shapely body, his tapering elegant hands.

When he'd first noticed me, first asked me to dine with him, I'd been flattered – any girl would be. Me, just a humble junior house physician being squired by the most eligible man on the hospital staff!

Almost without my noticing it, feeling flattered had changed to feeling excited. It had startled me, the way my heart would lurch when I saw him come into the wards or the out-patient clinics. I had started to watch for him, and when that first dinner date had been followed by another, and another, and then a visit to a theatre, I had found myself slipping fast into a state of bemused adoration.

And then, only a month ago, just before Dad's death, there had been that hospital dance. And afterwards he had driven me back to the hospital, and leaned over and kissed me goodnight before opening the car door, and I had melted with delight. He'd said nothing about how he'd felt for me, but I had hoped, perhaps one day – Any girl would have felt the same way.

But Dad had died, and I'd had to resign from the Royal, seek a better paid job in general practice, and Charles – had Charles really understood? Oh, he'd said we'd meet again, whenever I could come up to town, and said vaguely he'd try to visit me in Tetherdown when he could – but nothing definite had been arranged. So what would happen? Would he forget me?

I'll write to him, I promised myself. Just a friendly letter telling him how I am, asking after him, hinting delicately that I miss him – because miss him I knew I would. I did already.

The train slowed, rattled over points, and slid noisily into Fenbridge station, and I leaned forward to look out of the window, curious to see something of the area. This was the first time I'd been to this part of England. My heart sank as I saw the grim dirty buildings that flanked the big station, smelled the dust and smoke that filled the air. Would Tetherdown be as dingy as this? It was a hateful thought.

I leaned back in my seat, and stretched my legs wearily. I was tired already. The door of the carriage rattled and opened abruptly just as the whistle blew and the train started to move forwards and, too slowly, I pulled my legs back. Too slowly, because the man who got in fell sprawling across my feet to land with a painful crunch on the grubby floor.

"Oh, I'm so sorry!" I gasped, and jumped up to help him. The train was gathering speed now, and I lost my balance, so that I lurched and landed against him, just as he was getting awkwardly to his feet – and the poor man went headlong again.

I couldn't help it. I sat on the floor beside him in the lurching train and laughed aloud. He looked so silly, sitting there rubbing his head, and I felt so silly sitting beside him with my admittedly brief skirt rucked up, showing a great deal more of my white tights than any respectable doctor should.

He glowered at me, and got up, making no attempt to help me, and I scrambled to my feet and said again: "I *am* sorry – but it was funny, wasn't it?"

He brushed his hands over his dusty overcoat and scowled at me. He was a big man, with a craggy sort of face and broad hefty shoulders that made his coat look strained across his chest.

7

"Is it funny?" he snapped. "That's a matter of opinion. I find the humour of the situation escapes me."

"Brr," I said, a little pertly and with a mock shiver. "Have I upset your dignity? I can't do more than apologize, can I?"

He looked at me with such patent dislike in his face that I began to feel irritable myself.

"Anyway, it was as much your fault as mine," I said sharply. "If you planned things better, you wouldn't catch trains by the skin of your teeth – you'd be able to get on them with the dignity that seems to matter to you so much."

He opened his mouth to answer, and then snapped it shut again, and turned to pick up the big briefcase he had dropped as he fell over my feet.

"Women," he said over his shoulder, as he pulled open the door to the corridor. "You're not safe out without someone to keep you out of trouble. If you'll take my advice, in future you'll keep your long legs" – and he stared at my brief skirt with sharp disapproval written all over his face – "to yourself." And he slid the door to with a snap and disappeared along the corridor.

"Whew!" I said aloud, and then grimaced. If the rest of the people of the district were as sour-tempered as he had been, life was going to be grim indeed. Imagine having him for a patient! I let myself imagine the situation, me sitting in surgery ringing the bell for the next patient, and seeing that man march in. What would I do? I chuckled. Make him undress to be examined, I promised. That would soon puncture his precious dignity!

I looked at my watch. Twelve-thirty – the train was due into Tetherdown in another twenty minutes or so, so I took myself along the corridor to the washroom, tidied my make-up, and made myself look as neat as I could. Perhaps I should have worn clothes a little less fashionable, I thought doubtfully, looking at myself in the little mirror, at the Mary Quant coat over a culotte dress and white tights and bowed patent leather shoes. Maybe they'll think I look too frivolous to be a good doctor.

And then I put my tongue out at the mirror and said aloud: "Phooey! Begin as you mean to go on. I may be doing a dreary job, but it doesn't mean I have to look like a drear – "

When the train drew in, I waited a few minutes before pulling my luggage from the rack and getting out. I didn't want to bump into Sour Face again, thank you very much; and he might be somewhere in the corridor.

It was a small station, with just two lines, and as I dropped my luggage on to the platform, the train shrieked and pulled out again on its way further north, and I looked round curiously.

It was rather a nice-looking station, with a few late snowdrops growing in the flowerbed by the station master's office, and there was a clean country smell in the air. At least it isn't a dirty town, I told myself optimistically, and humping my bags, made my way to the exit.

Outside there was a wide cobbled yard with a couple of private cars parked in it, and a row of taxis. I just saw the bad-tempered man climb into one of them as I came blinking out into the sunshine, and fell back so that he shouldn't see me. So he did belong to Tetherdown, instead of further up the line! I giggled to myself. Maybe he would turn out to be a patient after all!

And then I heard a shout, and turning, saw a small black car coming into the yard, passing the taxi bearing my fellow passenger away. Dr Redmond was leaning out of the window, driving awkwardly with one hand as he waved at me. He drew up beside me, and got out, wreathed in smiles.

"Well, my dear, well, well! Sorry to be so late – hope I didn't keep you waiting too long, but I had to make a visit on the way – " and he began to load my luggage into the car.

"Oh, how nice of you to meet me!" I said. "You really shouldn't have bothered. I could have taken a taxi."

"Not at all, not at all!" he cried, busily helping me into the car. "Can't let you arrive in Tetherdown without welcoming you properly. Glad to have you, you know. Very glad to have you indeed."

He climbed in beside me, and started the car with a roar, and then we were off, going through the town at a breakneck speed. I peered out eagerly, trying to get some idea of what the place looked like. I got a brief impression of broad streets, lots of trees just showing the first tender green of spring, a wide central square dominated by a soaringly beautiful church, a busy shopping street, its narrow pavements crowded with people, many of whom waved at the car as we passed.

My spirits lifted, for this was a pretty town, clean and cheerful and not the dismal half-dead place I had feared it would be. I turned to Dr Redmond who had been chattering busily ever since we had left the station.

"– introduce you to the other partners," he was saying. "Hope you'll like them. There's just one small detail, of course. Perhaps I should have mentioned – oh, well, can't be helped. Thing is, I haven't told 'em much about you. They're good men, both of them, excellent men, but, well, you know how it is."

He peered at me a little vaguely and then returned

10

his attention to the road. "I – er I haven't mentioned that you're a girl, d'you see. I'm the oldest partner – the senior – but I've no prejudices about women in medicine – none at all. Wouldn't have appointed you if I had 'em, would I? No. But the other two – well, I just don't know. We've never discussed it, d'you see. But I daresay there'll be no problems. They'll be delighted to see you – delighted. We've been sorely overworked lately, what with the influenza epidemic, and the sudden rise in the birthrate."

He chuckled. "I swear we've had every young couple in the town deciding to enlarge their families this spring. The maternity side of the practice never stops! And with all those babies – well, that was the thing about you that most pleased me. We need someone who likes babies and children, understands 'em, d'you see. I'm getting too old for them, and Max and Peter – well – haven't the same touch you'll have, m'dear."

I began to feel better than ever. Not only a pretty town and a pleasant man to work with (for I was rapidly coming to the conclusion that Dr Redmond was a darling) but plenty of the sort of work I liked best. Perhaps life as a general practitioner in Tetherdown wasn't going to be too bad after all!

The car turned left, away from the busy town centre and then swung right into the driveway of a big house, built of soft red brick, with mullioned windows, and ivy growing along its broad walls. There were wide flowerbeds filled with shrubs and a few daffodils starred the lawn under a venerable beech tree. I warmed to the place at sight.

"And here we are at Downlands, m'dear," Dr Redmond said, drawing up with a flourish in front of the wide door, just alongside a taxi that was parked before it.

11

"I have a wing for my own use, the surgeries are here in the centre of the house, and the top floor is Peter's – Dr Cooper and his wife. Max – Dr Lester – he has the converted coach house for his home – "

He got out of the car, and I followed him, just as the taxi drove off, leaving its passenger on the doorstep. I stared at him in horror. It was the man I'd so unfortunately encountered on the train.

"Hello!" Dr Redmond said, surprised. "Where's the car?"

"Blasted clutch went – stranded me in Fenbridge. Had to take the train back," the big man said, staring at me with a marked frown between his eyebrows.

"Oh, bad luck," Dr Redmond clucked, his round old face creased in sympathy. "But I'm forgetting my manners! My dear – " He turned to me. "May I present my partner, Dr Max Lester?"

He smiled at Max and said: "Max, this is Dr Phillipa Fenwick, our new assistant. I'm sure you'll get on famously – "

Looking at the expression of horrified disbelief on Dr Lester's face, my heart sank. I wished I could be as sure of that as Dr Redmond, I thought ruefully, as I held out my hand to one of my new partners.

CHAPTER TWO

I sat in the Coopers' drawing-room, a glass of very good sherry in my hand, and listened to Dr Redmond bumbling on about the state of the practice, while I looked round and sorted out my impressions.

Max Lester was sitting sprawled on the window seat, staring gloomily out at the gardens, turning his sherry glass in his hands.

He'd brushed aside my renewed apologies for the incident on the train, had scowled alarmingly as I explained, in response to Dr Redmond's demands for understanding, what had happened. And when Dr Redmond had thrown back his white head and laughed uproariously as I described what happened (and I hadn't been able to resist being a little malicious, making more than I need of the absurdity of Max's position on the floor of the carriage) he had produced a wintry smile that he'd turned off like a light as soon as he could. Oh, undoubtedly, Max Lester wasn't a bit pleased at having a woman – especially one like me – joining the practice.

My gaze shifted to Peter Cooper, sitting beside Dr Redmond, his head bent attentively towards the older man. Now, he was far from sorry to see me, I decided, and then he looked up and caught my eye, and smiled broadly. I smiled back, noticing the way his face seemed younger when he looked relaxed.

He was a dapper man, fair and good-looking, about – oh, forty or so, I thought. I felt his eyes linger on me, and embarrassed, I looked away. I'm not conceited, but I know when a man thinks I'm attractive. And there was no doubt Peter Cooper approved of me in no uncertain terms.

My glance slid across to Judith Cooper, his wife. She was sitting on a low stool, her back to the wall by the huge stone fireplace where pine logs burned aromatically, her dark brooding stare fixed on me. She looked away as I caught her eye, at her husband, and then back at me again, and as clearly as if she had spoken. I realized that she too had noticed Peter's response to me.

I blushed suddenly and hotly, and cursed myself for it. It was absurd the way I coloured up like a child at the least thing. At my age, I should have grown out of it.

Judith moved, reaching for the decanter of sherry which was conveniently placed on a small table beside her. As she refilled her glass, Peter's voice cut across sharply, interrupting Dr Redmond, which surprised me. Peter Cooper didn't strike me as an ill-mannered man. If it had been Max Lester, now –

"Judith, how are we progressing towards lunch? I've got a clinic at two, I'm afraid, and time is running on – "

Judith drank quickly, emptying her glass at a gulp, and then got up, and moving in a rather slouchy way, went across the big room towards the door. The light from the wide windows lit her clearly as she passed them, showing the early lines on her face, the hollow cheeks and hint of scragginess about her neck. But she had a lovely figure, and I wondered why she looked so sulky. She couldn't be more than, what, thirty-five or so? Why did she seem so old and tired? Clearly, Judith Cooper was a person about whom I had a lot to discover.

"I'll see what's happening," she said huskily, and disappeared through the door.

There was a short silence, and then Peter Cooper said with a sort of forced cheerfulness: "Well, Dr Fenwick – "

"Oh, please," I said. "Don't be so formal – not if we're to work together. My friends call me Pippa – won't you? All of you?" and I looked round at the three of them.

"A charming short version of a charming name," Dr Redmond said. "And I for one am delighted to call you by it. But I'm old-fashioned enough to prefer being called Dr Redmond."

He chuckled. "Truth to tell, my first name is so ghastly I never use it," he said in a confiding tone. "Cedric! I ask you!"

Peter and I laughed, and then Peter said: "And my friends, Pippa, call me Peter. You shall too."

"Thank you – Peter," I said, and looked across at Max Lester, but he hadn't moved, and still sat staring moodily out of the window. Oh, all right, I thought. Be a misery if you want to. One of these days you'll get over your sulks, I suppose –

"– have you made any decision about where to live?" Peter was saying, and I turned and stared at him in consternation.

"Oh, my goodness," I said, and bit my lip. "I must have lived in hospital too long – I never thought about it! Just took it for granted that I'd live with the job. I'd forgotten this was general practice."

"And what's wrong with general practice?" Max Lester's voice cut across harshly, and I turned and stared at him.

"I beg your pardon?" I said.

"You speak as though general practice were something too lowly to be worthy of your consideration. Is that how you feel about it?"

"I don't think I sounded as rude as that!" I retorted, nettled. "Of course, I'm not going to pretend I regard general practice in the same light as I would my chosen speciality, but – "

"But it makes a tolerable second-best, is that it?"

"I didn't say that," I said furiously. "I only meant – "

"I can imagine what you meant." Lester stood up and stared at me with insulting chilliness. "You meant what all hospital-centred people mean. That general practice is a backwater, that all the worthwhile people are working in high-powered hospitals, and that only dreary also-rans like my colleagues and myself waste their time in it."

I reddened again – I couldn't help it. Wasn't that just what I'd been thinking in the train? But to hear it hurled at me in this way, in front of people who were devoting their lives to the job was deeply embarrassing.

"Now, now, Max, easy does it," Peter Cooper said, at the same time that Dr Redmond spoke, getting to his feet.

"Come on, Max, you need your lunch. Get you mounted on that hobby horse of yours and we'll be here all day – "

The awkwardness passed, and grateful to Dr Redmond, I stood up too. Peter Cooper came across the room to stand beside me.

"We still haven't solved the problem, though, have we? Where you're to live?" He smiled down at me from his six foot height and went on: "I must talk to Judith about this – "

"About what?" Judith's husky voice made me jump and turn away from Peter almost guiltily – which was silly, as there was nothing to feel guilty about.

She was standing by the door to the dining-room, staring at us. "About somewhere for Pippa to live in Tetherdown," Peter said easily. "Look, Judy, couldn't she have the turret room? It's standing empty, and why not have it used? If Pippa would like it, I'm sure she'd be excellent company for us – " and he turned and smiled at me.

I was still looking at Judith's face, and as Peter said "the turret room", it changed, seemed to sag and look suddenly old. But it was a passing thing, for then it settled again into its original petulant look.

"The turret room," she said, after a moment. "Yes. I suppose you're right. No point in leaving it empty any longer, is there?"

Peter looked at her and said, with an oddly gentle note in his voice, "No, Judy. None at all. So shall Pippa have it?"

"Why not?" and then she tried to smile, and I warmed to her a little. Whatever it was that made this woman so strange, I thought, it wasn't sheer nastiness. She's unhappy. And I was almost surprised at the thought.

"Yes, you shall have it," she said. "As Peter says, it would be company for us – we do get a little lonely sometimes – "

She crossed the room, and poured another glass of sherry for herself. "More sherry, anybody?" No one answered, so she drank quickly, and then said: "Well, lunch is ready. Come and get it while it's hot – " and she led the way into the charming small dining-room that overlooked the front of the house, with tendrils of ivy growing round the window frame.

17

Lunch was a pleasant meal, with good food well cooked. I ate hungrily, enjoying the lamb cutlets and crisp fried potatoes and broccoli Judith offered. There was cherry pie and fresh thick cream, and as we lingered over steaming hot coffee I sighed and said happily: "I did enjoy that. Thank you – er – Mrs Cooper."

"Judith," Peter said. "No formalities if you're going to be one of the family. Eh, Judith?"

"Of course," Judith said, and then without looking at me went on: "Would anyone care for a little brandy with their coffee? No? I think perhaps I shall – "

I noticed Peter's brows crack down sharply into a frown, and I suddenly realized what it was about Judith that had been at the back of my mind. Of course. She drank so much more than the rest of us. I'd had one small glass of sherry, as had Peter and Dr Redmond and Dr Lester. But she had had at least four brimming glassfuls, and now, brandy. Was this her problem, the cause of the oddness I had noticed about her? It seemed likely.

"I must get to my clinic," Peter said, putting down his coffee cup. "And you're doing the afternoon visits, Max?"

"Yes," Max said. "How many?"

"Barbara left the list on my desk. Help yourself," Peter said. "And you can use my car until yours comes back from Fenbridge."

1 With a muttered "excuse me" to the rest of us, Max Lester left the room, and I felt a good deal more comfortable once he'd gone. His disapproval of me had been like something you could touch, it had been so strong.

"I'll bring your cases up now, Pippa, and you can unpack later," Peter said. "Perhaps you'd like to sit in on my clinic this afternoon. Get the feel of the place, hmmm? That all right with you, Judith?"

"Yes – I suppose so," Judith muttered, and put her hand out to the brandy decanter again. I caught Peter's warning look at her and she dropped her hand.

"Well, I'm taking the afternoon off," Dr Redmond said, getting to his feet. "Old man's privilege. Going over to the Agricultural College to see my boy, Jeremy." He smiled at me. "You must meet him, Pippa, soon. Nice boy, though I say it myself. Image of his mother – pity she died before he grew up. Ah, well, water under the bridge, water under the bridge."

I thanked Judith for lunch, and tried to say how happy I was to be living with them – for indeed, the thought of having a room in this lovely house was much more attractive than having to find digs somewhere in the town – but she hardly responded, just sitting amidst the remains of lunch with a sulky look on her dark face.

Peter showed me to the turret room, which was indeed lovely. Perfectly round, with two deep windows facing each other, a pretty four-poster bed and delicate white and gold trimmed furniture.

"It's enchanting!" I said, as Peter set my cases down. "Fit for a princess in a fairy tale!"

Peter's face lost its relaxed look, and he stood very still, looking round. Then he sighed and said: "That was what it was meant for – "

I looked puzzled, and he said a little wearily: "We had a baby daughter. She would have been – almost nine if she'd lived. But she died at three months – meningitis. Judith, well, Judith hasn't been the same since. We knew she could never have any more babies, after little Emma

19

was born, and when – when she died, part of Judith died with her."

"Oh, I'm so sorry," I said, and impulsively put my hand on his arm. He smiled down at me, and closed his own hand over mine.

"It's sweet of you to be so sympathetic," he said. "Of course, it's not so bad for me. I've got my work, but Judith – she has nothing. She just sits, and broods – I've tried to persuade her to find some sort of outside interest, but there – she won't or can't. So – she – " he swallowed. "You must have noticed. Everyone does. She drinks too much. She can't help it, and it could be worse, I suppose. I mean, she's never – incapable."

"I'm sorry," I said again, and extricated my hand. There seemed nothing else to say.

He smiled again then, and said: "I'm glad you've joined the practice, Pippa. We need some young blood, and maybe – who knows? Maybe having you living with us will help Judith."

"I'll try to help, all I can," I said warmly. Then a thought struck me. "Look, Peter – won't – won't Judith hate it – having me here in this room?"

He shook his head firmly. "Even if she does, she'll have to learn to cope with it. She's made this room into a shrine, and it's just not healthy for her. No, it's right for you to be here. Just having you here will help."

I followed Peter downstairs into the surgery part of the house, feeling a little better now I understood Judith a little more. If only Max Lester weren't so horrid to me, life here could promise to be very pleasant.

As though he'd read my thoughts, Peter said over his shoulder: "You mustn't mind Lester's bad temper, Pippa, He's like that. He's a good chap at heart, and he'll come round to you, you'll see." He gave me another of his attractive smiles. "He won't be able to help it – you're a charming girl, and no one could sulk at you for long, even if he had been sent sprawling by you!" and, inevitably, I blushed.

As we came down the broad polished wooden staircase I looked round approvingly. The central hall of the house was big and warm, with a lively coal fire burning in the grate that almost filled one wall. On one side four doors bore labels, each with a doctor's name on it, and I was pleased to notice that one already had my name on it.

"That was used as a storeroom," Peter said, pointing to it. "But we fixed it up for you. I'll show you in a moment. Now here" – and he pointed across the hall – "is the waiting-room – full already I daresay." And I could hear people's voices coming from beyond the closed door.

"This room here is for Barbara, the secretary and receptionist, and beyond our consulting rooms there is a small treatment room. We're lucky – well equipped. It could be used as a minor operating theatre if we had to – though fortunately we never have. Now, I put your bag in your room – the medical bag I mean. The black one with the gold clasp."

I nodded. "Yes, that's my medical bag." My father gave it to me when I passed my finals, and for a brief moment I felt the familiar grief well up in me as I remembered the way his tired lined face had lit up when I unwrapped it. Dad had been a leather worker, a superb craftsman, and he'd made the bag for me during the late nights, tired though he had been after long days at his bench, earning a living for all of us.

"I noticed it specially," Peter said. "It's a beauty. Now – "

The door that bore Max Lester's name swung open, and Max came out, shrugging on his overcoat.

"Oh, there you are, at last, Cooper," he grunted. "Look, that Chesterfield child – what did you start him on?"

"Chesterfield? Um – let's see. Oh, the otitis media? I remember. I put him on tetracycline, six hourly – "

"Fine. If he hasn't responded, I'll arrange a bed for him at Fenbridge, right?"

"Fine. His mother won't be particularly surprised. By the way, Max – have you finished with the microscope? I might need it this afternoon," Peter said.

"Mmm. I put it in the storeroom," Max grunted, making for the door.

"The storeroom? You mean Pippa's consulting room," Peter said.

"Oh, do I?" Max looked back at me. "I suppose a store-room will make a perfectly adequate consulting room for Dr Fenwick. For the time being. I have no doubt we'll be calling it the storeroom again soon." And he went out of the big door, and then I heard the roar of a car engine.

"Ouch," I said softly, and Peter put his arm across my shoulders and gave me a friendly hug.

"Don't take any notice of the old bear," he said. "He's always a misery till you get to know him."

"Peter."

We both whirled at the sound of Judith's voice. She was standing on the stairs, looking down at us, and again I felt that absurd sense of guilt – and wondered if it was Judith's glowering face that made me feel that way, rather than Peter's easy comradeship.

"I wanted to do some shopping – may I use the

22

car this afternoon? I'll be back well before evening surgery."

"I'm sorry, Judy – Max took it. His own is stuck in Fenbridge until tonight. You'll have to do your shopping tomorrow." He looked up at her with an odd expression on his face, and I tried to analyse it. Irritation, affection, impatience, anxiety, they were all there. And something else I couldn't put my finger on.

"We really must start this clinic, Pippa," Peter said. "I'm late already. I'll see you at tea time, Judy – " and turning he led me into his consulting room, and rang the bell for the first patient.

It was an ante-natal clinic, and as each young pregnant woman came into the room, Peter introduced me and told me something of the history. There was a charming girl of twenty-four – just my own age – expecting twins, and I warmed to her when she said, "What's your first name, doctor?" and then said, when I'd told her, "Lovely. If one of the twins is a girl, I'll call her Phillipa. And if the other is a boy – why, I'll call him Phillip! Pippa and Pip – won't that be nice?"

"Lovely!" Peter said heartily. "And now let's have a listen to see how Pip and Pippa or whoever they are are getting on – "

And so the afternoon wore on, and I was so interested and happy in what I was doing that it came as a surprise when Peter stretched and yawned and said, "That's the lot for this week, then! Time for tea, and then evening surgery. Dr Redmond's taking that."

"Thank you for introducing me to the practice so pleasantly," I said sincerely. "I really enjoyed this afternoon. I'm looking forward to learning more about Tetherdown and the people I'll be looking after in it."

23

"Tell you what, young Pippa!" Peter said. "Tomorrow, come on visits with me. It'll give you a chance to see something of the town, and since I've got to finish up at our branch surgery in the afternoon, we'll get a chance to see some of the countryside too. What do you say?"

"Oh, that would be lovely! If Dr Redmond agrees of course – he may want me to do something else."

"No, he's leaving the planning to me these days – Max too of course, but mostly me." He got up and made for the door, standing back first to let me go in front of him.

"That's settled then – "

As I opened the door, the phone rang, and making a face he went back to his desk. Over my shoulder I said, "Indeed it is settled. We'll call it a date!" and I went out, leaving him to deal with the phone call.

And almost ran into Max Lester, who was standing outside the door, his face furious.

"Already?" he said, and his voice was so sharp I jumped.

"What do you mean?" I said, my voice showing my surprise.

"Making – 'dates' – as you call them. Listen to me, Dr Fenwick. This is a big busy practice. We need another doctor, not a flibberty fly-by-night miss who just plays at medicine. What we *don't* need is a disruptive influence, certainly where the Coopers are concerned. You've already reduced Judith to a state of misery – I just left her in floods of tears, and half drunk, because she's not stupid, you know. She saw the set you made at her husband, just as I did. Now, *leave him alone*. Get on with the job you came here to do – and as far as I'm concerned the sooner we replace you with a real doctor – a man who cares about the job and not his own social life – the better. You can be

24

sure I'll do my damnedest to see that happens *very* soon," and he turned on his heel, and ran up the stairs, leaving me shaking with temper, and confusion, and on the verge of tears.

I hardly knew where to turn. To be attacked in this fashion – it was hateful. Desperately, I looked round, and seeing the door with my name on it, pushed it open, and almost ran in, to lean against it on the other side, trying to regain my composure. And what I saw finally broke my control altogether.

There was a desk in the centre of the room, and on it was my lovely black leather bag – the one Dad had made for me so lovingly. But it wasn't the way it had looked when he had made it.

It was slashed into great gaping holes, its contents lying strewn on the blotter, the handle ripped off, a travesty of its original self.

I went over to the desk, and put out one shaking hand to touch it. It fell on its side, showing the interior. And there I saw that the red silken lining was ruined, smothered in black. Whoever had slashed the bag had emptied a full bottle of ink into it, too.

The door opened, and Peter came in, inquiry on his face. I looked up at him, and my control went, so that tears ran down my face.

"Who could have done such a thing, Peter? Who? Have I made someone hate me so much already? Who could have been so cruel?" I said piteously.

And Peter came and put his arms round me, so that I wept on his shoulder, letting out all the build-up of grief and anxiety that had been lurking in the background of my mind all day.

CHAPTER THREE

I can't pretend that my first evening in Tetherdown was a really enjoyable one. I excused myself from having dinner with Peter and Judith Cooper, pleading tiredness. The real reason was that I couldn't have faced Judith, not without blurting out what I was thinking – and that would have made things impossible for me at Downlands.

I was completely convinced that it was Judith who had damaged my bag, who had vented her half-drunken spleen on one of my most treasured possessions. All the evidence pointed to her. Her husband had displayed a liking for me that had verged on frank admiration. She must have seen me as a rival – an idea which was laughable. After all, I was more than half-way to being completely besotted with Charles, far away in London – but she didn't know about Charles of course.

And then there was the matter of the turret room. It was all very well for Peter to say it was high time the room was used, to try to lay the ghost of the baby Emma by installing me in her fairytale room, but how could he be sure that Judith had accepted the idea as readily as she had seemed to? Perhaps the thought of me in that room had been enough to push her over the edge of rational behaviour into the act of crazy destruction she had committed.

And then – she had collapsed into floods of tears. Why?

I had no reason to doubt that Max Lester had spoken the truth when he'd told me that Judith was upset and it was my fault. Whatever else Max Lester was – rude, bad-tempered, prejudiced – of one thing I felt quite sure. He was brutally truthful. He couldn't tell a lie any more than he could act one – which was why he was behaving so sourly to me. He disliked me and made no bones about it.

So it must have been Judith who had damaged my bag, for who else *was* there who –

And then I sat bolt upright in my bath – for that was where I had been lying in heaps of fragrant bubbles and thinking – and felt my head spin as another idea came swooping into it. I'd been assuming that the culprit had been Judith – but *couldn't* it be someone else? The only qualification a person needed was to dislike me – dislike me enough to want to get rid of me and not care what methods were used to achieve those ends. Couldn't that just as easily be Max Lester as Judith Cooper? In fact wasn't it *more* likely?

And then I shook my head and subsided into the bubbles again. No. This act of petty vandalism had been committed by a woman. I like my own sex but I have to be honest and admit that there are some women who can be very nasty in a way a man can't. And I couldn't imagine Max Lester standing over my bag with a knife in his hands. Or could I?

And so my thoughts went on, spinning like a squirrel on a treadmill. What with fatigue and distress and all that thinking I thought I'd never get to sleep, but I curled up in the little white and gold bed and tried to make myself think of nice things, like Charles. But that only made me miserable, made tears prick behind my closed eyelids. I tried to think about my brother instead –

He was standing beside me, ringing a handbell and crying monotonously "Lend me a fiver, Flip. Lend me a fiver – " And then I was awake and groping for the telephone on the bedside table. "Mmm?" I said sleepily, feeling as though I were still at the hospital and answering a night call.

"Pippa? This is Peter Cooper." The thin voice clacking at the end of the phone brought me back to the present with a rush. "Look, Pippa, I'm sorrier than I can say to do this to you on your very first night, but I've got to. Both Dr Redmond and Max Lester are out on a call – they're dealing with a tricky high forceps delivery at one of the farms – and I – I can't leave Judith at the moment. She's ill." He paused for a moment. "You understand what I mean, Pippa?"

Indeed I did. Judith must be in an alcoholic state of some sort. "Do you want me to come down?" I asked crisply.

"Lord, no!" he said. "I can cope with *her*. No, it's just that there's been an urgent call for a visit. A baby, from one of the cottages down on the north side of the industrial estate. It's difficult to work out just what the problem is, from the call. The mother phoned, and she sounded very upset – in a fearful flap. And then hung up on me! I think someone ought to go, and as I say, I can't – "

"Then of course I shall," I said, already out of bed and stretching to reach my clothes. "I'll dress and come down and you can give me directions."

I've had a lot of experience of dressing hurriedly for night calls, and I was downstairs and tapping at Peter's door within a few minutes.

He opened it and came out, and as he did I saw over

28

his shoulder into the room. Judith was lying sprawled on the bed, her face flushed, and breathing heavily. The room smelled stale and unpleasant, and Peter had a drawn look on his tired white face. He was still dressed, with his shirt sleeves rolled up, and as I looked at him, I felt a twinge of pity. Such a nice good chap, tied to a woman like Judith –

"Bless you for this, Pippa. It's rotten to have to take a night call when you don't even know your way around the town – "

"Forget it," I said. "The sooner I start real work, the sooner I'll learn about the practice. Where do I go?"

He gave me clear brief instructions, and I nodded as I repeated them to fix them in my memory. Then Peter said, "You can take my car – here are the keys. And you'll find my spare medical bag in the boot. I always keep an emergency set there. You use it until we can get yours repaired."

As I let myself out of the house I shivered a little. It was cold, but not too dark because a late moon was just dropping towards the trees on the west side of the town. The car started easily, and I swung it out and into the main road, turning left as Peter had instructed.

Even though I was concentrating on the journey I had a chance to take in some of the passing scene, and I soon realized that I was leaving the pretty part of the town behind, leaving the wide streets and trees and snug sizeable houses for a much poorer section. The houses became small and terraced, and even in the fitful moonlight I could see that here cleanliness and neatness didn't matter nearly as much as they did in other parts of the town.

I lost precious minutes looking for the street Peter had given directions to, but at last I spotted the sign high on the side of one of the houses. Paradise Street. Not very heavenly, I thought wryly as I noticed the grimy windows, and paint peeling from doors, and the garbage piled in the gutters. The house I was looking for was the very end one, flanking the railway line, and as I swung the car round the corner, past the telephone kiosk – the call must have come from there, I thought automatically – a train rattled and roared past the end of the street, drowning the sound of the car completely, making so much noise I could hardly hear myself think.

I had parked the car at the edge of the dirty pavement and was standing on the doorstep by the time the train had rattled away into the distance and silence returned to the dingy little street. I raised my hand to knock, and then stopped as I heard muffled voices.

There was a deep one, a man's voice, and it sounded harsh and angry, though I couldn't make out the words he was using. Then there was a softer feminine voice, and this one sounded as though it were pleading, somehow – and then the thin wail of a baby cut across, and I nodded to myself. No doubt about it – this must be the house.

I knocked on the door and the voices stopped immediately, and even the baby's cry stopped in mid-wail, as though it had been switched off. I waited, puzzled. Surely having sent for a doctor they must realize that was who was knocking? And I knew there was someone awake to hear me. Why didn't they answer? I knocked again, louder, thumping the rusty knocker against the cracked wood with a long rat-tat, but still there was no answer.

I stepped back, and stared up at the house, but all I could see were blank shuttered windows, with grimy curtains pulled secretly across them, and not a glimmer of light showing through.

I paused, hesitantly, and then I heard it again – the wail of a baby, cut off sharply, as though someone had put a hand across its mouth –

Quite suddenly, I was angry. Furiously angry. I had been called out of a warm bed on a chilly night, sent traipsing around a strange town in answer to an emergency call, and now I was being left standing on the doorstep like a bailiff or something instead of a doctor. And on top of that somewhere in this house there was a baby, a sick baby – for the sound of its cry, high pitched and thin, told me that – and someone was ill-treating it. That was all I needed to make me lose my temper.

I flung myself at the door and beat furiously on it, shouting at the top of my voice.

"Open this door – do you hear? Open it at once! I'm a doctor and I've come to see that baby, and unless you open the door I send for the police! Now, *let me in*!"

Down the street I felt rather than heard or saw front doors open, heads peer out, and a bit of me was amused when all of them disappeared when I said the word "police".

From within the house there were sounds, scuffling sounds, and then I heard a rush of footsteps, and the door creaked and opened, letting a little light from the hallway spill out on to the pavement.

There was a girl standing there, quite a young girl, not much older than myself, though she looked desperately tired and ill. Her thin fair hair was pulled back and fastened with an elastic band on the top of her head. She had a pale drawn face, and an expression of sick anxiety made it look even more tired and ill. She had an old cotton dressing-gown pulled round her, holding it with one transparently thin hand.

31

"What – who is it?" she said huskily.

"Dr Fenwick," I said briskly. "Dr Cooper couldn't come himself, but I'm the new partner in the practice – " I stepped forward, to enter the house. "Now, where's this baby of yours?"

But she pushed the door to, peering round it in terror and said breathlessly, "No – no, don't come in. I mean – he's fine. I – I made a mistake, you see. Yes, that was it. I made a mistake. I thought he was ill, but now I know he isn't, so I'm sorry to have bothered you, so please – *please* go away before he comes down – "

"Before *who* comes down?" I asked, puzzled, and tried to peer round the edge of the door. "I don't understand – anyway, now I'm here, I might as well see your baby, just to be on the safe side."

I could still remember hearing that thin high-pitched cry, and it worried me. The last time I'd heard that sort of sound it had been made by a baby with a brain tumour. That type of cry is called a cerebral cry, because it indicates that something is wrong inside the skull somewhere – and I had no intention of leaving this house until I knew why that hidden baby had cried like that.

I pushed against the door, but the pale fair girl pushed back, and said again urgently, "*Please* go away. Please – "

And then the door was flung wide, and the fair girl was thrust away to stand shrinking against the wall, and a man stood there glowering at me. He wasn't particularly big or burly – in fact he was a fairly scrawny sort of chap, with a thin unshaven face and bony arms – but the impression of sheer violence that hung about him was so strong that I stepped back in alarm.

"Listen, lady, you heard what she said, didn't you? You got ears, haven't you? So use 'em – and get going. We don't want you here, not now nor ever, so go and poke your nose in other people's business and leave us alone – "

And the door slammed violently in my face and I was left on the doorstep staring up stupidly at the house.

I raised my hand to knock again, my anger bubbling up to overcome the very real fear the man had created in me, but a voice behind me made me whirl.

There was an old woman standing there, the light from her own open front door, across the street, glinting on the metal curlers in her sparse grey hair. She was wearing a heavy woollen coat over a nightdress, and men's slippers on her elderly feet.

"Don't you go knocking again, lovey, not if you values yourself," she said earnestly. "He's a right horror when he's roused, that feller – you'd really best be off, you know. Not that that baby shouldn't have seen a doctor today if you ask me, poor little scrap of a thing, but there it is. Anyway, he's in good hands, the baby I mean – Dr Lester's looking after him – "

"Dr Lester?" I said.

The old lady nodded. "Oh, yes. Little Mrs Higgins, she takes the baby to see Dr Lester when the old man's out, so he shan't know, you see. So he's in good hands – "

"But that baby ought to be seen *now*," I said. "I heard his cry, and I'm worried – I'll have to get into the house to see the child – "

"I'd send for Dr Lester if I was you, deary," the old woman said. "A slip of a girl like you – you can't manage a nasty job like Higgins. You send for Dr Lester – "

"I can't," I said, "he's on a maternity case – I'll have to manage on my own – "

"The new partner, are you?" the old woman said, and grinned at me. "I heard what you said to Mrs Higgins.

Well, you'll have your work cut out, won't you? What with Dr Lester and all – " and she giggled. "Doesn't think much to women doctors, does Dr Lester, as well I know. Heard him going on once I did, at that young woman as came out from Fenbridge hospital to help in the epidemic last winter, and ooh, he was nasty – "

"Really?" I said icily. "I can't say that interests me much at the moment. Right now I've got to get into that house and see that baby, and if Higgins or whatever his name is won't let me in, then I'll get hold of someone else who'll make him."

"Like who?" the old woman said curiously.

"Like the police," I snapped, and turned on my heel and marched down the street towards the phone box.

I heard the old woman behind me call out, "I wouldn't do that, deary – Dr Lester wouldn't – " but I took no notice. I couldn't care less about Dr Lester, or his opinions of women doctors, or how he would have managed the problem now facing me. All I knew was that I had to get into that house, somehow, and see that baby. And if in the doing of my job I managed to show Dr Lester that I was a capable woman and as good a doctor as he was – well that would be pleasant, I'm woman enough to want to show off sometimes!

I slid into the rather smelly phone box, and breathed a sigh of relief to see it was in working order. So often telephone kiosks were ruined by vandals – but I was in luck. As I didn't know the telephone number of the local police station, I did the easy thing and dialled 999. They put me through to the police with commendable speed, and I explained as crisply as I could what the situation was, and asked for help.

"It's a bit difficult, doctor," the voice at the other end of

34

the line said dubiously. "We can't just break into people's homes without just cause you know, or a warrant – "

"Isn't a sick baby just cause?" I snapped. "I'm afraid that baby is very ill and will come to real harm if he doesn't get medical care fast. Surely that's enough authority?"

"Well, I suppose so – " the policeman said. "Are you the family's regular doctor?"

"No – I mean, in a way," I said. "That is, I'm a new partner in Dr Redmond's practice at Downlands. I understand Dr Lester usually sees the child – but he's out on a difficult maternity case up at a farm somewhere – "

"That'll be up at White Gables," the voice at the other end of the phone cut in.

"I've no idea where. Anyway, he's out, and I answered this call in his place. And now I'm not prepared to leave the house until I see that child. Will you or will you not help me? I tell you that in my medical opinion this child ought to be examined – "

"All right, doctor, all right! I'll send a car right away. Just you stay there, and my men'll assess the situation when they get there – meantime, I'll try to contact Dr Lester," and the phone went dead.

I stood on the pavement outside the telephone kiosk simmering with anger. Dr Lester, Dr Lester! The way people in this town went on you'd think Dr Max Lester was the only doctor that ever existed. How dare that policeman decide to contact Dr Lester over my head?

It took the police car a good ten minutes to arrive, and by that time I was in a state of barely controlled anger. I was furious with the Higgins man, furious with myself for not being able to get into the house without sending for help, and above all furious with Dr Lester, just for being Dr Lester.

The two policemen in the squad car were young, and one of them said cheerfully "Morning, doctor! Won't be long now, I hope. Sergeant's sent for Dr Lester, so he should be here soon – "

At that my control snapped completely. "Dr Lester has nothing to do with this situation! I'm the doctor in charge at the moment and what I say goes! And I say we are going to get into that house right now, because there is a baby who is dangerously ill in there and I am determined to see him *at once*. So come on – "

The two policemen looked at each other, and the driver said doubtfully, "But the sergeant said – "

"I don't care what the sergeant said!" I snapped, almost dancing with rage. "We're going into that house, and we're going in now – so come on – "

And I marched up the narrow little street, now lined with open doors and windows as people peered out to see what was going on, leaving the policemen to follow.

The next ten minutes or so were blurred with action, as far as I was concerned. As I reached the house, the policemen coming reluctantly behind me, the door flew open, and Higgins came bursting out – and to my horror he was holding a wicked-looking length of heavy wood in one hand.

"You interfering, wicked, nosy – " and he let forth a stream of abuse that made me whiten, even though in my early years in hospital, when I worked in casualty departments, I'd heard a lot of bad language.

I backed up, scared, and Higgins came for me, still swearing and waving his wooden club. I caught a brief glimpse of his frightened wife as she scuttled out of the house, holding a bundled shawled baby, and fled to the old woman across the street, who put a protective arm

36

round her. Then, the policemen were there, in front of me, holding on to Higgins with a grim effort as he struggled to get at me and shrieked and cursed at the top of his voice.

And then, his wife came running round, leaving the baby in the arms of the old woman, and tried to talk to him, while the policemen struggled to control the man, now almost incoherent in his fury.

"She didn't mean no harm, Pete, honest she didn't! But the baby *is* ill, you know that, and I couldn't get Dr Lester not any way, and they sent her instead, but she meant no harm – " Mrs Higgins said, tears running down her face as she looked up at her struggling furious husband.

"She sent for the police, didn't she?" he bawled at her. "Didn't she? Means no harm? Like hell she don't! Thinks she's going to get me put away again, does she, sending for police? I'll show her. Just you let me get at her and I'll show the – " and he struggled against the policemen's brawny grip so hard that he almost managed to get away and the watching neighbours shrank back against their front doors, and I stood almost mesmerized with fear.

"Higgins! Stop that right now!"

The voice wasn't particularly loud, but it had such great authority that somehow everyone stood frozen for a second, and even Higgins stopped pulling against the grip of the two policemen.

I managed to turn my head, and saw Max Lester standing just behind me, with a police sergeant beside him. Max's eyes slid over my face with a chilliness that made me shrivel. Then he spoke very softly.

"Since it seems to be you that is making my patient so – distressed, the sooner you get out of his sight the better. Go back to the end of the road and into the police car."

I stared at him, and then managed to speak. "Your

patient? You mean him?" and I jerked my head at the man now standing still, almost drooping, between the two policemen. "I'm not concerned about him – it's the baby I came to see, and the baby I shall see," and I turned on my heel, and started to march across the street with my legs shaking with reaction from the fear that Higgins had created in me.

"Come back here!" Max said harshly, and reached out a long arm and grabbed my elbow. Then, he seemed to become aware of the staring little crowd that was clustered around us, and turned and glowered at them.

"Go back to bed, all of you. This is nothing to do with you, and the sooner we get a bit of peace and quiet here the better. Now, on your way."

And so firm was his authority that obediently the crowd melted away, and doors closed behind dressing-gowned and overcoated figures, and windows closed, and still Higgins stood there drooping, the very opposite of the raging fury he had been so short a time before.

Max Lester looked at Higgins and said gently, "Pete."

The man raised his head and stared at Max Lester's face, which now had a gentle expression on it that made him look completely different from the way I'd ever seen him look before.

"Hello, Dr Lester," he said, and his voice was flat and dull.

"There was no need for all that, was there? If the baby was ill, Jenny was right to send for a doctor, now wasn't she? You'd be miserable if anything happened to the baby, wouldn't you? Of course you would. Now listen to me, Peter. There's nothing to fret about, do you hear me? Nothing at all. But I think the baby ought to be in hospital for a while, and – "

And then it happened again. Before our eyes, the meek drooping Higgins changed, became again a raging, flailing, shouting creature, and managed to pull away from the policemen who had been holding him, to fly at Max Lester.

For a moment I was terrified, thinking Higgins was going to attack the big man, but Max just stood there calmly, only putting up one arm to ward off the attack.

"Stop it, Pete," he said softly – and Higgins stood still again, staring up at Max.

"You're not going to put me away, and you're not going to put my kid away neither," he said in a surly voice. "I knows *you* means well, but her – " and he stared venomously at me, "she's the bad one, wanting to get the police here and take my kid away. You get rid of her, you hear me, or no one goes near that baby, not nohow – "

Max didn't turn his head, he just spoke very softly.

"Dr Fenwick. Please will you go to the police car at the end of the road? I'll take Dr Cooper's car, and talk to you at Downlands shortly."

For a moment I wanted to argue, and then realized that there had been an odd pleading note in his voice. Max Lester, not only speaking to me politely – even addressing me by name – but pleading! I was so surprised that almost before I realized what I was doing, I was walking down the street next to the police sergeant, and getting into the big black car that stood, with its blue light turning on the roof, at the end of the road.

I wanted to wait, to see what was going to happen, but the police sergeant just shook his head at me and nodded to the driver and in no time I was back at Downlands, standing on the doorstep and watching the police car disappear down the drive. But I had to know what had happened, and Dr Lester had said he'd explain at Downlands later – so, I let myself into the house, using the door key Dr Cooper had given me when I left on the emergency call, and switched on the hall light.

The house was completely silent. I stood in the middle of the elegant quiet hall, looking round at the gleaming polished surfaces, the flowers in their low bowls on the tables, the silent closed consulting room doors, and suddenly I was very, very tired. But I wasn't going to bed until I knew what had happened to that baby. So I sat myself on the bottom step and leaned my aching head on the banisters.

I must have fallen asleep, because suddenly, he was there, and I was staring up at him stupidly. How long he'd been standing there I don't know, but he still had his coat on, and was holding his soft crumpled hat in one hand.

"What – what happened?" I asked.

"Nothing very bad, fortunately – but no thanks to you!" he snapped.

I stared up at him, at the crease between his eyes, the uncompromising set of his mouth, and my tiredness and the anxiety of that half hour outside the Higgins' house added up to a total that made my own temper snap.

"Dr Lester, don't talk to me in that fashion! It's abominably rude, and I've done little to deserve it. Now, either you tell me what happened in this case, or you don't – but at least do me the courtesy of telling me why you're displaying so much hostility and anger towards me!"

He looked startled, and then rubbed his eyes with one hand.

"Yes. I suppose you're right. You're entitled to know what you nearly did – " He looked very directly at me then, and said, "Higgins has been a patient of mine for just over

40

a year. He was discharged from a mental hospital as being reasonably under control – but since the baby was born three months ago he's become much worse. I've managed to treat him with drugs, and psychotherapy – finding time to talk to him, to let him talk – and I was getting on quite well with him. He had two main obsessions. One was about being locked up – the mere mention of the word police drives him wild, because it was the police who first got involved with him, took him to court, and the court referred him for a medical opinion and then discovered his mental illness. So, he blames the police for the fact he went to hospital, and not his own illness. And when you threatened to send for the police, *and then did*, you made his control snap completely. Especially since you're a woman."

"What's that got to do with anything?"

"He hates women doctors – it was a woman psychiatrist that the court arranged for him to see, so policemen and women doctors are about equal villains in his eyes. And *you* turned up at his house tonight, and threatened to send for the police if he didn't let you in! Do you wonder he finally went berserk?"

"But that's ridiculous!" I said. "He couldn't have known who was at the door when I first knocked, but they didn't answer! It wasn't till I told his wife that he could have known who I was – "

Max Lester shrugged wearily. "It doesn't matter now. He *did* run berserk, as you saw, and it was sheer luck that he didn't hurt someone. I've got him into Fenbridge hospital now, and heavily sedated, and we'll see where we go from here. My guess is that you've set him back months with your meddling. If you hadn't gone off half cocked and sent for the police he'd have calmed down, and – "

41

"For God's sake, Dr Lester!" I nearly shouted it at him. "I didn't know any of this! I was sent to see a sick baby! Dr Cooper told me nothing of the father's history – just that there was a sick baby to be seen. And I heard the child cry, and it worried me. He had a cerebral cry, and – "

"Oh, for heaven's sake!" Max Lester looked disgusted. "You specialists! You can't accept a simple possibility – always got to look for some complicated diagnosis. I spoke to Jenny after you'd gone, and she said she sent the call only because the baby had been sick, and she was sorry to have made such a fuss over nothing. And you hear a baby cry once and immediately diagnose a brain tumour or something, I suppose! Such nonsense – "

I flushed hotly. "It was not! I know I only heard the baby cry twice but it *was* a characteristic cry, and I believe I was justified in trying every way I knew to see the child! Anyway, what's happened to him? Where is he now?"

"At Fenbridge hospital. I took them there myself – all three of them. Jenny Higgins can stay there with the baby till tomorrow, when I daresay they'll send him home, *cerebral* cry and all – "

There was a sudden buzzing sound, and I whirled, startled.

"The phone," Max Lester muttered, and went across the hall to his own consulting room, switching on the desk light as he reached for the receiver.

"Yes? Lester here. What? Baby Higgins – yes. Yes – " He listened for a long time, and his face altered, showing first surprise and then a sort of sick acceptance.

"I see," he said heavily. "I see. What? No. It was my – my colleague, Dr Fenwick who suspected it. Yes. I'll tell her. And I'll see she comes in to see the baby tomorrow – I mean later today. Yes. Goodbye." And he cradled the receiver and stood there with his head bent for a moment before looking up at me.

"Well, I owe you an apology. The baby – he's got a fractured skull. That cerebral cry you heard – it was a true bill. Jenny Higgins has admitted that – that her husband attacked the baby this afternoon, and that was how he was injured. You were right and I was wrong. I thought I could help Peter Higgins stay at home, and I was wrong. I'll arrange for him to go back to the mental hospital for further treatment tomorrow."

He sighed heavily, and again rubbed his eyes. "I'm dead on my feet." And then he looked up at me again, and behind the tiredness I could see the old implacable look.

"But I must be quite straight with you, Dr Fenwick. You made the right decisions on the basis of slender evidence in this case tonight, but I believe that was more a fluke than due to a mature medical judgment. I still believe that you are the wrong person for this practice, in every way, and will do all I can to replace you at the earliest opportunity. Good night."

And he walked past me, and went through the green baize door that led out to the covered way to his converted coach house flat, leaving me staring after him in the silent brightly lit hallway of Downlands.

CHAPTER FOUR

Peter Cooper and I had breakfast alone, since Judith didn't feel well enough to get up. Peter told me this heavily, and said no more about her, although his tired shadowed eyes and pallor showed he'd had as disturbed a night as I had.

I told him, very briefly, about the case he'd sent me on, and when I said it had been the Higgins' baby, he groaned.

"Oh, no! Pippa, I'm so sorry! If I hadn't been in such a – a flap last night, I'd have recognized the address, and never have sent you. Higgins hates women doctors – "

"I know – now," I said grimly, and told him the rest of the story, but leaving out the harsh things Max Lester had said. I was still smarting under the injustice of his attitude, and somehow I didn't want to talk about it, not even to sympathetic Peter Cooper.

"Anyway, the whole thing's under control, now," I said. "Dr Lester says he'll have the father admitted to the mental hospital again for further treatment, and the baby is under care at Fenbridge. I'd like to go in later today and see him, if that were possible. What's on the agenda for the day?"

"Morning surgery is at nine thirty," Peter said. "And usually we all meet at nine, just to plan the day. Dr Redmond should be there by now" – he glanced at his watch – "so we might as well go down."

"What about Judith? Will – will she be all right on her own?" I asked, a little nervously. I didn't want to sound inquisitive.

"Mrs James – our daily help – will take care of her. She's already in – she made breakfast. Did you think I had?" He laughed. "I don't know what we'd do without Mrs James. Don't worry. She'll get Judith on her feet by lunchtime, and the place cleaned up, and lunch organized. She always does – " and he led the way out of the flat and down to the consulting rooms.

I felt a deep surge of pity for him as I followed his neat figure down the stairs. Living with a woman who drank as heavily as Judith must be hell, I thought. But he accepts it all so calmly, even the fact that he has to rely on his daily helper to "get Judith on her feet". It's all wrong, I thought protectively.

Dr Redmond was sitting in his consulting room, which was the biggest of the four, with Max Lester sitting on the window seat. He merely looked up and nodded as Peter and I came in, but said nothing. Dr Redmond, however, was full of chatter.

"Good morning, my dear! I've been hearing all about your baptism of fire last night – too bad, too bad. These things happen of course, they happen. I told Max right from the start that he was asking for trouble trying to manage a case of paranoia as severe as Higgins', in his own home. The man needs constant hospital care in my opinion, but not to fret, not to fret. The Fenbridge people tell me the baby's doing well, doing well. They operated on him in the small hours, they say, removed some blood clot from the brain, and the outlook is excellent. They've transferred him to the neurosurgical unit – "

"Oh," I said, a little disappointed. "Does that mean I

won't be able to see the child? A pity. I'd have liked to, very much. I didn't get a chance to examine him last night, and it would have been interesting. Still, now he's had surgery there wouldn't be much to discover, I suppose – "

"Are you interested in the child as young Gary Higgins, or as a medical case, Dr Fenwick?" Max Lester's voice was deceptively soft.

"What?" I said, startled. "Oh – as a medical case, I suppose, though as a person too – "

"There lies the difference between us, Dr Fenwick, I'm a GP – a family doctor. I care for my patients as people *first*, but as cases of medical interest second. I'd recommend you do the same – it makes a great deal of difference."

"Now, Max, leave her be, leave her be. She's young and we all had to learn, didn't we?" Dr Redmond said. "Now, to work. Where's Barbara? Not in yet?"

Peter, who had stretched himself out on the consulting room couch, laughed lazily.

"My guess is she's making the first of the day's coffee. That girl thinks we need coddling like babies," he turned to me. "She brews gallons of coffee, all day long. You'll see – " And as though on cue, the door opened, and a girl came in, balancing a big tray on one small hand. She was very pretty, with red gold hair and huge blue eyes, and a tiny neat figure.

"Good morning, doctors," she said softly, and put the tray down on the desk before starting to bustle with cups and milk and sugar.

"We must introduce our newest partner," Dr Redmond said. "This is Dr Fenwick, Barbara. Barbara Moon is our prop and stay, Pippa. She sorts out our appointments, plies

46

us with coffee, copes with the phone, soothes irate patients – a complete treasure I assure you."

"Oh Dr Redmond," Barbara said, dimpling. "How you do go on, to be sure," and I heard the pretty lilting accent of the district. "Hello, Dr Fenwick. It's nice to meet you – " and then she went over to Max Lester and gave him a cup of coffee.

I couldn't help noticing the way she lingered over him, the look in her eyes as she turned away, and I thought, a little surprised, She's in love with him – But Max Lester hardly raised his head, and she moved away, disappointed.

Peter, however, made much of her, pinching her bottom in a joky avuncular fashion that made her squeal, and made Dr Redmond beam for all the world like a jolly Mr Pickwick.

She gave me my coffee then, and this amused me a little. Clearly in Barbara Moon's eyes I was very much the junior partner, and was to be treated as such. No old-fashioned rules about "Ladies first" here!

"I was sorry to hear about the damage to your bag, Pippa," Dr Redmond said, as Barbara tidied the coffee tray. "I can't imagine how such a thing happened – "

"Or *who* could have been so vicious towards Pippa – " Peter said.

I looked across at Max, just to see what sort of reaction he would show, but he was still staring moodily out of the window, and didn't seem to hear the conversation going on behind him.

"I can only suppose one of the patients – " Dr Redmond said worriedly. "But why? And who?"

"You never can tell with patients," Barbara said. "They can do all sorts of things – "

"Anyway, no point in going on about it now, I suppose," Peter said, "We'll send your bag to Daniels, Pippa. He's a leather worker – a great old character. Got his little place in the Square, and if anyone can fix it, he will. I've got to visit old Mrs Quale next door this afternoon, so I'll take it in to him then."

"That's very kind of you, Peter," I said, and smiled at him, and Peter grinned back and said, "For you, my dear, nothing is too much trouble," and blew me a mock kiss, which made Dr Redmond chuckle.

But Max Lester and Barbara Moon showed no sign of being in the least amused, and I found myself reddening as I looked across at Max and caught the sardonic look in his eyes.

"Now, work, all of us," Dr Redmond said, opening the big diary on his desk. "Barbara – when the patients come in, will you give the notes of new ones, or new visits after a long gap, to Dr Fenwick? Then she'll be able to build up her own group of patients while we deal with our own repeat visits and so on. Now, after that, visits – I'll take you with me, Pippa. I want you to get to know my visiting round, because frankly I want to ease up on visits. I'm getting older, and one of the reasons you're here is to make life a bit easier for me – so the sooner I show you the ropes, the sooner I can get lazy, hmm?"

It was extraordinary how quickly I slipped into the routine of the day. By the time I'd seen my first half-dozen patients I felt as though I'd been in general practice at Downlands for a month instead of for a day.

I enjoyed the afternoon, too, the visits to old people, and young mothers, and middle-aged housewives, cementing my impression of Tetherdown as a pleasant, pretty town.

We finished the afternoon's rounds just after four, and

Dr Redmond said, as we went back to the car from our last call, "We'll have tea at the College, hmm? I've got a boy I could see there – it'll save a visit tomorrow morning, and I'd like you to meet Jeremy."

He chuckled as he let in the clutch and swung the car out into the traffic. "If I get boring on the subject of Jeremy, you must tell me. I'm an old man, and he's my only boy – born late to our marriage, I'm afraid, and his mother died when he was still just a child – so I'm a bit wrapped up in him, as you can imagine. But he's a good boy, though I say it myself."

And indeed, Jeremy was a nice boy. We found him in the cattle sheds, after seeing the boy in the Sick Bay, who had an infected finger following an injury in the market-garden section of the College.

"Why is Jeremy here?" I asked Dr Redmond, as we made our way across the extensive College grounds towards the cattle sheds. "I mean – why did he choose agriculture for a career? Didn't medicine attract him?"

Dr Redmond shook his head. "No – and in a way he was pushed into this. His mother inherited a very snug little farm from her father, and in turn left it to Jeremy. He comes into full ownership of it at twenty-one – three years from now – so he decided to really learn how to run it! He'll make a good farmer, I think – got the feel for it."

As I say, Jeremy was a nice boy – tall and fair, and with a pleasant open way with him which made me warm to him. He cleaned himself up quickly, and changed from his working boots and overalls, and escorted us both into the College dining hall for tea.

It was a magnificent room, high-ceilinged and panelled, and the tea provided was delicious farmhouse fare –

home-made bread, and preserves, and scones with rich cream as well as jam.

"It's as well I don't eat like this every day!" I said, laughing at Jeremy. "I'd be hideously fat if I did – "

"You could never be hideous," Jeremy said gravely, looking at me approvingly. A *nice* boy, I thought again, so like my own brother David, and smiled warmly at him.

"Well, bless you for that!" I said gaily. "After last night and the lack of sleep it entailed, I'm lucky I don't look like my own grandmother!"

"And that must be our cue to go," Dr Redmond said, and stood up reluctantly. "This young lady needs some rest, and you have to get back to work, I daresay. I'll see you again soon, Jeremy – "

"Of course, Dad," Jeremy said, and put an arm round the older man's shoulders and hugged him briefly. "There's the dance on Saturday week remember." He turned to me then.

"Could you come, Dr Fenwick? It's our annual spring do, and great fun. I'd be very happy if you could join our party – "

"An excellent idea, Jeremy," Dr Redmond said approvingly. "Of course you must, Pippa. We're making up a party from Downlands – we're all going, the Coopers, and Max Lester, and Barbara Moon – and now you too."

"I'd love to, Jeremy. Thank you for asking me," I said, turning to the boy. "And you must call me Pippa if we're to be friends – Dr Fenwick sounds so – starchy, doesn't it? Goodbye until Saturday week then – "

On the way back to Downlands, driving through the pleasant countryside with its gently rolling fields and neat woods and cosy farmhouses, I found myself telling Dr Redmond all about David, just a year younger than his

Jeremy, and what a worry he was to me sometimes with his impulsive ways.

"He's a good boy at heart, you see," I explained, "but he doesn't always think before he acts – and he's shockingly extravagant, too."

"Boys – they're always a worry of some sort," Dr Redmond said soothingly. "Take my Jeremy, now. Hard-working, and certainly not extravagant – you'd think he'd give a father no worry. But he does, he does. Very shy, you see, shy. Never goes out with girls, to the best of my knowledge, and never kicks up his heels at all. I tell him – I'd like to see him marry young and make a grandfather of me before I die, but there – "

"He didn't seem all that shy to me!" I said, laughing.

"No – and glad I was to see it!" Dr Redmond said, and leaned over and patted my hand. "A nice sensible girl like you could be a real help to him. Take him out of himself, don't you see."

"Dr Redmond, I'm seven years older than he is!"

"My dear, I'm not match-making like some old country wife! Of course not. But if you could be friendly to the boy – teach him how to socialize – well, I'd be a grateful old man – "

"Not so old!" I said, and he laughed too.

Anyway, I promised him I'd try to "bring Jeremy out of his shell" as he'd asked, although I wasn't quite sure how he expected me to do it, and for the rest of the journey we talked about the practice and the town, and I found myself getting more and more fond of my senior partner.

For the next few days, things were busy but quiet at Downlands. I took surgeries of my own, went out on visits, finding my way around the town surprisingly easy, and getting to know the running of the place. I learned quite a lot about the people of Downlands, too.

I discovered, for example, that Dr Redmond was universally liked by the patients, and, surprisingly, that the least popular with them was Peter Cooper. I decided that this must be due to his sometimes abstracted manner – and that this in turn was due to the complications of his life with Judith.

It was also a little surprising to discover how many of the patients adored Max Lester. Several, when shown into my consulting room by Barbara Moon, in fact flatly refused to be seen by me, making it very clear that as far as they were concerned Max Lester was the only doctor in the world they would consider. Not that I was short of work, for I found that the word had gone round the town very rapidly, and several patients, mostly older women and young mothers, specifically asked to see me.

I also learned a little about Barbara Moon. She had always worked for the doctors of Downlands, ever since leaving the children's home where she had grown up. She was an odd girl, alternately friendly and confiding and sharp and withdrawn. She was as volatile as a child, and I could never be sure how I'd find her at the start of each day.

But by the end of the first week, I did know what made her tick – the way she felt about "her" doctors. She seemed to have poured out on to the three men every atom of feeling she had, the feelings she had probably been unable to express for anyone during her growing-up years in the home. Dr Redmond she treated as she would a father, Peter Cooper as a cheeky older brother, and Max Lester – clearly the way she felt about him was very complex and very deep.

I was more than ever convinced that she was in love with him.

As for Judith Cooper – I saw her every day, but made no progress at all towards getting to know her. Sometimes she appeared at breakfast, but more often she didn't, and Peter's face would tell me, with its weary pallor, that she had had another bad night.

Every evening she sat silently beside the fire watching television or listening to records, while Peter and I chatted desultorily over her head.

Certainly nothing was ever said about my occupancy of the turret room, and I told myself optimistically that she had accepted me. If it had been she who had damaged my bag (which Daniels had managed to repair beautifully, I'm glad to say), doing so seemed to have exhausted her malevolency.

So, by my second Friday in Tetherdown, I felt really at home, and was happy – as far as Tetherdown went. I'd written to Charles – a light-hearted friendly letter – but I'd had no reply yet; still, I told myself, he's a busy man. I'd also written to David, and had two letters from him, both asking, with beguiling charm, for a short-term loan. Loan, I thought ruefully, as I wrote out a cheque for him. Some loan! I'll never see this again!

But, as I say, I was happy. The thought of staying in general practice for three years wasn't nearly as agonizing as it had been. Until that Friday afternoon.

I came in from my visits, gratefully closing the front door behind me, to keep out the chill of an unexpectedly cold snap that was shrivelling the early April flowers with frost. As I rubbed my chilled hands together in front of the hall fire Max Lester's door opened sharply, and he came out into the hall.

"Dr Fenwick!" he said, and his voice was icy. "What is this I hear about your authorizing Gary Higgins' transfer back to Fenbridge hospital from the neuro-surgical unit?"

"Oh, yes!" I said. "They phoned this morning. They needed an urgent cot at the neuro unit, and wanted us to take over Baby Higgins' care at home. I told them that because of the social conditions he'd have to stay in hospital for a while and suggested they should transfer him back to Fenbridge – "

"Quite forgetting, I suppose, that his father was still a patient at Fenbridge? That he hadn't yet been transferred to the mental hospital because they have a bed problem?"

"I did forget that, yes," I said. "But what difference does it make?"

"Oh, none – none!" Max Lester said sarcastically. "Except that Higgins had just begun to calm down, apparently. But when his baby – and of course the baby's mother – came back to Fenbridge hospital, he saw them. It was inevitable he should – the children's ward runs parallel with the male medical ward where he is, and they share the main corridor. Anyway, seeing them was all he needed to get him all stirred up again. They've just phoned me from Fenbridge. Higgins has disappeared – walked out of the hospital, and gone God knows where. A dangerous man, a desperately ill man, and now he's wandering round the countryside in a rage. Because of you!"

"That's not fair!" I flashed at him. "How on earth was I to know first that Higgins would be so disturbed by the sight of his wife and child, and second that he was likely to see them? I don't know the geography of Fenbridge hospital! To blame me for – "

He turned on his heeel. "There is absolutely no point in discussing this any further. I'm going to Dr Redmond now – and I'm telling him that he'll have to make up his mind one way or the other. Either you go, and go now – or I do."

I went after him, furiously. The prejudiced injustice of this man! We reached Dr Redmond's consulting room door together, but it was Max Lester who opened it first and marched in. I was right behind him, and nearly ran into him when he stopped short, and I heard the sharp hiss of his breath as he stared across the room.

I looked over his shoulder, and then I too gasped and rushed past him to run across and fall on my knees beside the crumpled figure that was lying on the floor beside the desk.

Dr Redmond's face was suffused with a bluish tinge, and he didn't appear to be breathing. I fumbled for his wrist, trying to find a pulse, and then looked up at Max Lester. My own voice shook and seemed to come from a great distance as I spoke.

"He – he's not – I can't find a pulse."

Max was beside me then, and ripping open the clothes across the old man's chest.

"It's a coronary – I warned him it could happen – get the emergency resuscitation tray, and get it fast. We may be able to do something – "

CHAPTER FIVE

How long it really was I don't know, but it felt like an eternity. We worked over the inert body of Dr Redmond like people possessed. At some point in the proceedings – just as I was drawing up a syringe full of stimulant, I think – Peter Cooper came in, and took over the artificial respiration from Max.

Then it was Peter and I working, making the old man breathe again, forcing his heart to beat again, while Max frantically got through to Fenbridge hospital to arrange for an immediate admission.

And all the time I worked, I remembered Dad, and how we'd failed with him, how another attack suddenly coming so soon after the first had finally snuffed out his life, and I prayed the same thing wouldn't happen to Dr Redmond, to whom I had become very close during my short weeks at Downlands. After about five minutes he opened his eyes and looked up at me, a puzzled look in their blue depths, and he tried to speak.

"No – don't talk," I said softly. "You've had an attack, but you're fine now – but don't talk, don't make any effort at all. You know the drill, don't you?"

And he managed a weak smile that made my own eyes suddenly smart with tears, so trusting was it.

The ambulance, with a highly trained resuscitation team

aboard, came screaming up to the door a few minutes later, and within minutes, the flap was over. Dr Redmond was safely on the way to Fenbridge, leaving the three of us standing shakily in the hall, watching the tail lights of the ambulance disappear down the drive.

There was a sound behind us, and I turned, and saw Barbara Moon standing in the shadows of the staircase with tears running unchecked down her cheeks.

"It's all right, Barbara," I said gently, going over to put my arm round the girl's shoulders. "He's got every chance of recovery, now – "

And she gulped, turning her head to rest it on my shoulder, and wept even more bitterly.

"Don't, Barbara," I said. "Please – you'll only make yourself feel dreadful – and it won't help – "

"You did a great job, Pippa," Peter's voice cut across, and I looked up, surprised.

"What?"

"You did a great job," Peter repeated. "Have you used resuscitation methods like that before?"

I nodded. "At the Royal – yes. And once – once for my father. We – failed that time."

"I'm sorry," Peter said. "It doesn't always work, of course – but it can, in the right hands. And yours certainly are. I congratulate you – and us. You're a real asset to the practice. And my God, it's a good thing you're here. Not only did you help save Dr Redmond – you're here ready and able to take over all his work too – "

"An asset to the practice? Am I?" I said, and my voice was very even, as I looked across at Max Lester, who was still standing by the open hall door staring out into the garden. "Does Dr Lester agree with you?"

He came across to us then, closing the door against the dwindling light of early evening.

"I have no choice," he said harshly. "We can't run a practice this size with only two of us. It was getting heavy for three, which was why Dr Redmond took you on in the first place – not that – well, that's beside the point now."

He stopped and looked at me, and at Barbara who was still weeping into my shoulder.

"Barbara, for heaven's sake stop that caterwauling. It helps nobody – " and then he looked very directly at me.

"At least you aren't howling," he said, and his voice was a little less cold. "And I have to agree – you worked very well in that emergency. I couldn't have started resuscitation so promptly on my own – and it was the speed that saved him – "

And suddenly, Barbara was crying even more loudly, almost hysterically.

"Oh, for heaven's sake!" Max said impatiently, above her noise, but Peter shook his head at him, and came across and prised loose Barbara's grip on me, and took her to sit beside him on the bottom of the staircase.

"Now, what is it, Barbara? Dr Redmond's in good hands now, and there's every chance he'll do very well. So why the fuss, hmmm? What's upsetting you?"

The crying redoubled, and I looked, puzzled, at Max.

"Surely you guessed," he said irritably.

And then Barbara said, gulping, "The bag – Dr Fenwick's bag – I'm so sorry – I didn't – and if it hadn't been for her, Dr Redmond – " and a fresh burst of sobbing drowned her words.

"My *bag*?" I said, softly. "It was *Barbara*?"

"Who else?" Max asked, in equally low tones. "It was obviously Barbara – it's typical of the sort of thing she's likely to do, under stress. And she saw you as a potential source of stress. As soon as it happened I realized it was her doing."

"Why didn't you tell me?" I said. "Surely I had a right to know? As it was, I thought – " I stopped then, and reddened.

"What did you think?" He sounded genuinely curious.

"I –" I looked across to Peter and Barbara, who were now talking together softly, and then moved away. Max followed me.

"I thought at first it might be – Judith," I said in a low voice.

"A logical thought, I suppose. But despite her problems, Judith isn't as unbalanced as all that – while Barbara is."

He stopped, and then said, "You thought at first it was Judith, which means you thought of someone after that. Who?"

"I thought it might be you," I said baldly, after a moment.

He stared at me for what seemed a long while, and then smiled. It was very startling to realize it was the first time I had ever seen him smile, and it made an incredible difference to his face. He looked younger and friendlier and altogether a much more likeable person.

"Did I seem as hysterical a personality as that?" he asked. "I wouldn't have thought anyone, in their wildest moments, could see me doing something so typically adolescent – *feminine* adolescent – as committing a piece of wanton destruction."

"I didn't see it as hysteria," I said. "I saw it as an action designed to make it thoroughly clear I was unwanted here. And you'd made it very obvious *you* didn't want me here."

"For logical reasons, not for merely emotional ones, like Barbara's. I want the practice to have a hard-working level-headed man in it. Women are fine, in their place – but I don't believe medical practice to be one of them. So, I didn't want you here and made no bones about it. I still don't – but I've no choice but to make the best of things as they are. All I ask of you now is application to work, and some common sense. For God's sake don't do anything like transferring a patient, as you did this morning, without making quite sure it's the right thing to do. Up to a point I can see it wasn't entirely your fault that it happened – I've got a hot temper and I let it cloud my judgment – but you were still wrong. The Higgins family are a problem, and they're my pigeon. You should have checked with me – I was here, after all."

"Yes," I admitted. "I should have checked with you, under the circumstances. I suppose I didn't think. I assure you that I will think, however, in future. Will that satisfy you? Because if it doesn't, you'll just have to get someone else to help you and I'll go. I don't think I could work in the sort of atmosphere we've had around here – "

He nodded. "I agree. I told you before, and I'll tell you again. I wanted to be rid of you while there were three of us who could have coped with the practice. Now Dr Redmond's out of commission clearly we can't do without you – and extra doctors aren't that easy to find at short notice. So, you're necessary now. And since you are, I can assure you you'll have my full co-operation in all medical matters – as long as I can have yours."

"Of course," I said a little stiffly. "I'll consult you or Peter whenever necessary."

He held out a hand, and after a moment, I did the same, and we clasped and shook hands, a little solemnly.

"That's understood, then. And now I'm going to get some tea before starting evening surgery. I'd advise you and Peter to do the same."

He turned and walked back across the wide hall to Peter and Barbara, who was now looking a lot less upset.

"All right, now, Barbara?" Max said, and patted her shoulder briefly. "I daresay we can forget all about it now – hmm, Dr Fenwick?" and he looked over his shoulder at me.

"Of course," I said, and smiled at Barbara. "My bag has been mended, made almost as good as new, so I don't feel nearly as bad about it as I did. I think I can understand why it happened – people do things when they're – upset – that they wouldn't normally do."

Barbara nodded eagerly, and came across to me, and held out one hand rather shakily.

"I'm sorry," she said. "It was just – I don't know – you looked so young and pretty and all when I got a peep at you the day you arrived, and I thought my doctors wouldn't like me any more, with you to talk to, and it made me so mad, I just – "

"I know," I said soothingly. "I know. But of course 'your' doctors still want you. I do, too, and I'd love it if you looked after me as well as you look after them."

"I'd like to," she said, a little shyly.

"Good!" Peter said heartily. "Then make us some tea before we all dissolve into tears. All this emotion is making me positively weak at the knees – "

And we all laughed – even Max, a little – and Barbara bustled away to the little kitchen looking a lot happier, while the three of us went into Dr Redmond's consulting room to clear up the resuscitation equipment, and then to reorganize the work of the practice, for without Dr

61

Redmond to take part of the load the pressure was obviously going to be very heavy indeed.

And the succeeding weeks proved just how heavy a load the practice carried. As the days lengthened and the air softened with the coming of summer, the work piled higher and higher. A flu epidemic in the last week of April led straight into a measles epidemic that spread over the town like wildfire. Next year, Peter and Max and I told each other wearily, we'd see to it that every child in the town was inoculated against the disease.

But, I was happy in my work. Max Lester treated me with a professional courtesy that made a refreshing change from his original surly hostility, though he remained as chilly as ever in a personal sense.

But Peter – Peter was marvellous. He was kind to me, fun to be with, reliable to work with. Of course he was abstracted sometimes, especially after one of Judith's "bad nights", but I understood these, and never took his remoteness personally.

It helped that the news about Dr Redmond was good and remained good. He had to stay in hospital, which was a pity, because it would have been pleasant to have him in his own flat where we could visit him easily, but the senior physician at Fenbridge wouldn't hear of such a thing.

"He's doing well," he told us. "But let him come back to Downlands and what guarantee have we that he won't start trying to work again? No. I don't trust him – he's a shocking patient, however good a doctor he is. I want him here right under my eye."

We saw a lot of Jeremy, however. He'd taken to coming to Downlands frequently, on his way back from visiting his father at Fenbridge, and would sit and talk to Peter and Judith and me, up in the Cooper flat, long into the evenings.

I must confess that sometimes I found him rather boring; let's face it, he was so very *young*. But I wouldn't have hurt his feelings for the world, and knew how pleased his father would be to know his son was learning to be more sociable.

And, because of Dr Redmond's illness, we'd had to let poor Jeremy down over the College spring dance – so the least I could do was put up with a little boredom on his behalf.

One thing that pleased me was to see what a good effect Jeremy had on Judith. At first, when he sat and chattered at us, she just sat sunk in her usual apathy, but after a few such evenings I noticed she was joining in, becoming more animated. She somehow became protective towards Jeremy, defending him hotly in any discussion between himself and Peter in which the latter seemed to be doing best. She was, in a way, maternal in her attitude to the boy, and it was good to see it.

And then, my own private life took a turn for the better. I'd written to Charles twice, and hadn't thought much about the delay in any answer from him, mainly because I was so busy – not because I didn't care whether or not I heard from him, because care I certainly did. And then out of the blue, one morning in the middle of surgery Barbara Moon called me to the phone for a private call.

"Yes?" I said, a little impatiently, because I'd had to leave a patient undressed on the couch, waiting for examination. "What is it?"

"Phillipa!" The voice sounded very close indeed, and the warmth in its familiar depths made my whole body shiver and then seem to melt delightedly. "Phillipa, how good to hear your voice! How are you, my dear?"

"Oh – I'm fine, Charles, fine! And you?" I said a little breathlessly.

"Never better, my dear. Horribly busy, of course. I've just taken a suite of rooms in Harley Street – and private practice keeps one hectic. That's why I haven't answered your charming letters. Time is just impossible – but I've thought of you, of course."

"Have you?" I said, almost in a whisper. "I'm glad."

"In fact, I'm thinking of coming down to see you in this hell hole in which you've buried yourself – what is it called – Tetherdown? Is it too ghastly for you, my dear?"

It was extraordinary the sudden wave of affection and loyalty that swept over me, the slight sense of indignation that anyone who didn't know the town should speak so slightingly of it.

But all I said was, "No – it's not too bad." I couldn't really see myself defending Tetherdown to someone so sophisticated since I had been completely London-centred myself.

But Charles was coming to see me! That was more important than anything else. I tried not to sound as eager as I felt as I went on talking.

"It would be lovely to see you, Charles. When can you come? One weekend, perhaps? I'm sure we could put you up here at Downlands."

"Could you? That would be nice – so much pleasanter than some fearful country hotel run by clodhoppers! How about the weekend after next – the last week in May, that will be?"

"Fine," I said. "Just fine. I'll fix it up, and arrange to meet your train if you let me know – "

"I'll drive, my dear, so much more comfortable. I'll be down in time for dinner, hmmm? Looking forward to seeing you."

"Me too, Charles," I said ungrammatically but letting all the pleasure I was feeling spill over into the words. "Me too – "

And I went back to my patient in such a dream of delight that he, a rather wicked old man with a sharp tongue, cackled with laughter and poked me in the ribs, and asked me if the spring had got into my blood. And I had to laugh back and say that perhaps it had – for certainly I was feeling on top of the world at that moment.

I thought that two weeks would never pass, so much was I looking forward to see Charles. I arranged with Dr Redmond, the next time I went to visit him, to put Charles up in his flat for the weekend, and Mrs James, the Coopers' very obliging daily help, promised to clean the little flat and have it all ready. She seemed very impressed to be having a Harley Street consultant coming to stay, as indeed was Peter Cooper.

"What's his speciality, Pippa? Maybe we can pick his brains while he's here – get a few difficult patients for him."

I laughed. "Don't do that, Peter – he's here for a break, remember? Anyway, I don't think we've anyone in the practice who'd really interest him. His speciality is dermatology."

"Skin diseases!" Max, who was sitting in his favourite window seat (we were taking a well-earned morning coffee break) snorted. "What a speciality!"

"What's wrong with it?" I asked indignantly. "It's a very interesting field – and patients can get very distressed by skin disorders."

65

"Oh, I know, I know," Max said, a rather sardonic glint in his eye. "But you've got to admit it's a pretty cushy number! Consultant dermatologists work office hours, practically. They never get called out in the middle of the night or at weekends, because there are never skin emergencies, and if they go into private practice, like your Charles, they can make a great deal of money from patients rich enough to pay for their treatment."

"He's not 'my' Charles, as you call him," I said a little childishly. "And I think you're wrong. Charles didn't become a determatologist because it's a 'cushy number' – horrible expression! He's genuinely interested – "

And Max shrugged and turned away to read the *Lancet*, clearly losing interest in the discussion, leaving me feeling a little puzzled at my own reaction. Why should I care what Max – or anyone else for that matter – thought of Charles? It was my feelings that mattered, no one else's, yet here I was feeling decidedly put out by the note of disapproval in Max Lester's voice. Would I never get used to this man's dour ways?

The two weeks seemed to go very slowly, as I said, but just three days before Charles was due to arrive something happened which managed to drive even him out of my mind.

I was taking evening surgery, and I was on my own because Max was out on an emergency call, and Peter was having a well-earned evening off – he'd taken Judith into Fenbridge to see the repertory company do a performance of *Hedda Gabler*. Even Barbara Moon wasn't there – she had a foul cold, so when the surgery was half-way through I sent her home, telling her I could manage fine on my own.

The last patient – or so I thought – had just left, and I

66

stretched luxuriously, thinking greedily about a hot bath and supper on a tray in front of the fire – for Judith had promised to leave a meal ready for me – when the door bell rang.

I can't deny I swore softly. If that's another patient, I told myself as I went across the hall to answer it, turning up late for the surgery, I won't see them. I just won't – not unless it's *really* urgent.

I opened the door and looked out into the thin dusk, and the smell of hyacinths from the flowerbed in front of the house filled my nose with spring, made my senses stir, and somehow made me even more impatient with this late caller.

"Well, who is it? What do you want? Surgery hours were over almost an hour ago, you know – " I said – well, snapped, really.

A figure moved in the shadows, and then came into the light thrown by the open front door. It was a girl, dark-haired, slight and pretty – but with a face that was white and drawn, her curly hair stuck in tendrils to her sweating forehead. She was clutching a heavy and voluminous winter coat around her, even though the night was pleasantly warm and as she stood there looking at me, my irritation disappeared and became urgent concern.

"What on earth – " I said, and then moved forwards to catch her, just in time. For she pitched forwards into my arms in a dead faint.

CHAPTER SIX

I half carried her, half dragged her into the consulting room, for she was taller than I was, and surprisingly heavy. She began to come round from her faint by the time we got there, and was able to co-operate with my attempts to get her coat off and her on the couch.

Just as I got her coat off, she suddenly groaned and doubled up, and cried out in a voice thick with terror, "No – no – make it stop – please, make it stop – "

She stayed bent for a moment or two, and then let me move her, sit her on the couch, swing her legs up until she was lying down – and then I could see her properly, for the first time.

She was pregnant, though not really obviously so. Rapidly, I undid her clothes, and ran my hands over the gently coned abdomen.

I felt the baby move under my fingers, an experience I had had many times but which never failed to move me. About thirty-six weeks pregnant, I judged – just a few weeks from the time when the baby would be born.

I felt the abdomen harden under my fingers as a contraction of the muscle walls of the uterus pushed against the baby, and again the girl on the couch cried out in fear and tried to curl up, away from my exploring fingers.

"Just relax, my dear – just relax," I said automatically.

And with one eye on my watch, and my hand still on her abdomen waited to see what would happen.

And just one minute later, another spasm contracted the muscle wall, and again the girl wept and cried –

"How long have you been in labour?" I asked urgently, leaning across the girl. But she just shook her head, keeping her eyes closed, and turned away from me.

"Look, you *must* tell me – how long since this started?" and I put all the authority I could into my voice.

She moved her head restlessly, as another contraction came, but she didn't cry out this time, just holding hard to my hand instead.

"It doesn't hurt so much now I'm here," she said in a small husky voice. "I'm not so frightened now I've come – I should have come before, then it wouldn't have hurt so much – it was so awful, and there was no one there, no one at all – "

And again she rolled her head on the pillow, and whimpered slightly as yet another contraction pulled her slight body.

I loosened her hand, and moving rapidly, began to sort out from my instrument and dressing cupboard the things I'd need. This girl was in advanced labour, and would clearly deliver her baby very soon – there was no time to be lost. I had to assess how far on the labour was, and get ready to bring the baby into the world, premature though it clearly would be.

As I worked, setting the sterilizer going, scrubbing my hands, finding mask and gown and gloves, I talked to the girl, more to keep her spirits up than to get information.

"Who's been looking after you?" I asked.

"No one," she whispered. "No one at all. I couldn't go home, could I? Not like this. They'd have thrown me out anyway – so I just had to manage alone. All alone. Just me, and the baby – I used to talk to him, pretend he could hear me – "

She stopped, and took a deep breath, crumpling her face with effort.

"Good girl," I said swiftly. "Deep breaths now, easy and light – that's it – there! That wasn't so bad, was it?"

She opened her eyes and looked at me in wonderment. "No, it wasn't – not a bit. It just felt – I don't know. Strong, but nice – "

"That's because you've relaxed," I said gently. "Childbirth needn't be painful, you know – as long as a mother relaxes and stops being frightened, she can enjoy it."

"Yes," said the girl. "I was frightened – terribly frightened. I didn't know what to do, you see, when it started. Last night, in the middle of the night it was. Not much at first – but then it got more, went on getting more, and this morning I thought – the baby's coming – and I can't ask for help, and what shall I do – and I was so frightened – "

"Nothing to be afraid of now," I said. Then, gently I explained to her what I was going to do.

"I want to examine you, to see just how near to being born the baby is. Just relax and breathe deeply and it'll be fine – that's a good girl – now, just relax – deep breath – *that's* it – "

I moved fast after that. My examination told me that the labour was very well advanced indeed, and that any minute now, this girl, who had been so frightened but now seemed a little more relaxed as she held on to my hand trustingly, would start to push her baby into the world. And there were things I had to find out about her first – about her medical history and the care she had been having during her pregnancy.

"Which hospital were you booked into?" I asked gently. "Tell me that, and your name, and I'll get in touch with them for some information before the baby arrives. Just tell me that much – I promise I won't tell anyone about you – "

For I realized she wasn't married, and had been hiding herself from her parents all through the long months of waiting.

"No one," she said, shaking her head, and looking up at me with wide amber-coloured eyes.

"I told you – there was just me – me and the baby, in that little room. I've been working in a factory – until last week – and they never knew. I told them I'd always been fat, and I wore a big apron, and they never knew about the baby coming – "

And I could see how easily she could have deceived people, for the baby was small – my first examination of her had shown that – and first babies are often easy to conceal, even well into the eighth month of pregnancy.

"And then tonight I couldn't bear it any more, so I went out. And then I saw the names at the gate – doctors' names. And I knew I couldn't do anything more on my own. I was so frightened – and so lonely – so I rang the bell. I'm sorry to be a nuisance – "

"You aren't a nuisance, silly girl – never that. I just want to know about you. Do you mean you've had no ante-natal care *at all*?" I spoke as gently as I could.

And again she nodded, and closed those beautiful eyes as another contraction came, and she grasped my hand in small cold fingers.

Now I was desperately worried. It was worrying enough to have a girl in advanced labour land on my doorstep in this fashion – but much worse to discover that she had had no care at all during her pregnancy.

No blood tests, no urine tests, no watch kept on her blood pressure – this could be bad. She was probably anaemic, for she wouldn't have been feeding herself properly all these long lonely months, and certainly hadn't been taking the necessary iron pills.

Childbirth, I knew, was safe these days, safer than crossing the average busy road – but for a girl who had had no ante-natal care there were risks, real risks, and I knew it.

And I was alone with her, and any moment now she would start to push her baby forwards towards the moment of birth. And I wouldn't be able to leave her side, even to use the telephone to get help.

And even as I realized this, she started. She took a deep breath and set her teeth, and her face lost its pallor and started to redden as she made the first efforts towards helping her baby to be born. There was no time at all to spare for telephone calls – only time to hold on and help her.

Those next minutes were extraordinary for me. Part of me was scared – just as scared as the girl herself had been when she arrived. But part of me was exultant, for to be there when a baby is born is a great and exciting thing, and one that never fails to fill me with excitement and joy and – yes – a little envy, envy of the girls lucky enough to be performing the supremely exciting and glorious task of giving birth to a baby.

And then, the baby's head appeared, the face crumpled and with a comical expression of rage on it. And the girl on the couch gasped again, and took another great breath, made one more final effort, and then – the baby was in my gloved hands, the little arms flailing wildly, the mouth opening hugely in a lusty bawl.

The girl on the table turned and looked at the baby in my hands, her face creased with wonder and doubt and excitement all at once.

"It's a girl!" I cried. "A beautiful girl – with dark hair like yours – "

A small baby – if she weighed five and a half pounds I'd be surprised, I thought, but a perfect baby in every way.

Swiftly, I wrapped the baby up, and made sure she could breathe easily before lying her down in a drawer of my desk which I had hurriedly emptied on to the floor, before lining it with a towel. I tipped the head of the drawer on a couple of books so that the baby would be able to breathe without any obstruction.

And while I worked, the girl behind me whispered "Emma. Her name is Emma – my little Emma. No one shall ever – "

And then, just as I was ready to turn away from the baby, to go back to the new mother on the couch, there was a gasp and I whirled. Was the after-birth coming already?

But it wasn't that. It was the one fear I had had at the back of my mind ever since I had realized that this girl had had no ante-natal care.

The big danger in these neglected cases is eclampsia, in which the mother has violent convulsions – and can die. And the girl on the couch was having a convulsion.

I did all I could. I used every technique I had been taught to use in such emergencies, but nothing I did seemed to help. Convulsion after convulsion tore at the fragile body, while the baby, the baby she had called Emma, lay and cried with a healthy noisiness behind us.

And then, above the sounds the girl on the couch was

making, and the mewing of the baby I heard another noise – the front door.

"Max!" I called frantically. "Max!"

And it was him. I saw his big frame come through the door with such gratitude that for a moment my head was spinning, and then he was beside me, and taking in the whole situation at a glance, pushed me to one side and took over.

My hands were shaking as I turned to look at the baby, whose tiny starfish hands had escaped from the towel in which I'd wrapped her, and were waving about furiously. She was a good pink colour, and tiny though she was, was clearly a very lusty child. Nothing to worry about here.

But what about her mother? I turned back to look at her, moving to see round Max's broad back –

And realized with a sick certainty that the very thing I had feared had come to pass.

This girl, little more than a baby herself, had been left alone to struggle through the months of pregnancy unaided, unloved – and above all uncared for. And because of this neglect, the normal safe experience of childbirth had been converted into a tragedy.

For the girl on the table was dead. Baby Emma, so newly born, was already without a mother, and the realization made me so angry, so furiously impotently angry, that I stamped my foot, for all the world like a child in a rage, and tried to speak, and couldn't, only bursting into hot tears of misery and fury.

Max took hold of my shoulders, shaking me a little to make me regain my control, and waited quietly until my tears subsided.

"I'm sorry," I said after a while. "I couldn't help it. It – it's such a wasteless *stupid* tragedy – she'd had no ante-natal care, you see. I managed to find out that much. She just turned up on the doorstep, almost in the second stage of labour, and I couldn't do a thing but deliver the baby – God, Max!" I cried out, "I didn't even get time to find out the poor girl's *name* – "

"You saved the baby, anyway," he said, and the matter-of-factness in his voice did more to bring me back to control than anything else.

"It seems a pretty lusty infant. In these cases it's touch and go whether you lose the baby as well as the mother, sometimes."

"I know," I said. "I suppose that is something. If *only* she'd gone to someone for care – if only – "

"No point now," Max said practically. "You say you don't know the girl's name?"

I shook my head. "There wasn't time," I said simply. "Only time to deliver the baby."

I laughed then, a little hysterically.

"I know the *baby's* name. She called her Emma. But before she could say anything else, she started to have convulsions, and then you came – and there's nothing else to tell. It all happened so *quickly*. And oh, it's so senseless, so wickedly senseless, a tragedy – " And again tears pricked my already stinging eyelids.

There was a sound from the hall again, and then footsteps. Peter and Judith, back from the theatre, I thought dully, and turned away from the door. I didn't want them to see my red swollen eyes, to know I had lost my professional control and wept for this tragic little mother's wasted death.

"Hello, you two! Working late?" Peter's voice sounded breezy, and then changed.

"My God – what's happened here? Is that girl – "

"Yes," Max said flatly. "She just died, poor little scrap. We've no idea who she is, or where she came from – nothing at all – "

"Don't even know her name?" Peter sounded incredulous.

"No," I said wearily, turning round. "Not even her name. Only her baby's. She called her Emma before she died – "

"Emma? Did you say Emma?"

And then I realized that Judith was in the room, was standing with her back to the door staring across at the desk drawer on my consulting room table, her face white with shock.

I don't know why I did it. I'll never know why. But very deliberately I walked across the room, and picked up the baby in her hand towel wrapper.

"Yes, Judith. Emma. The same name as the child you lost. That's the name this baby's mother chose for her – and she needs looking after." And I carried the baby across the room and put her into Judith's arms.

For a moment Judith stood there, frozen, staring down at the bundle she was holding stiffly and awkwardly. Would she reject her, throw her back at me and storm out of the consulting room to drink away her memory of the grief that had been caused by an Emma, so long ago?

But then she relaxed, and her arms crooked easily and gently and she lifted the child to set her own cheek against the tiny streaked cheeks in the time-hallowed gesture of motherhood. And the baby snorted softly and stopped crying, slipping into the sudden sleep of the very young.

Judith turned, and walking in an almost dreamlike state crossed the hall to the stairs, and carried the baby up them, disappearing from our view as she reached the landing.

76

There was a long pause. And then Peter spoke.

"Oh, my God, Pippa. Have you any idea what you've done? Any idea at all? The cruellest thing, the cruellest, wickedest thing anyone could do – "

"No," I said, and shook my head. "You're wrong, Peter. I'm sure you're wrong. You've tried to protect Judith all these years, keep her away from babies – but she *needs* to look after one, needs it desperately. It's because that need isn't satisfied that she drinks, I'm sure of that – "

"Are you?" Peter said. "You may be right. But have you thought of what effect it will have on her when she has to *stop* looking after that baby? Because she'll have to, you know. She won't be able just to *keep* her. Things don't work out that way."

I stared at him. "But if no one claims the child? All I managed to find out about that poor little mother was that she was alone – no one knew about her pregnancy. The only people likely to claim this child are the Children's Welfare people from the local council. And you know as well as I do that they're only too happy to leave a baby in someone's care if that person can be shown to be fit to do the job – "

And then I stopped.

"Precisely," Peter said, and his voice was filled with despair.

"Precisely. Judith – my wife – is an alcoholic. She's the last person who would be considered suitable to care for a child, even though she's a doctor's wife. Don't you think I've thought of something like this before? I'm not completely stupid, you know!"

He stopped then, and rubbed one gloved hand over his face, with a weary gesture that made me want to look after him as though *he* were a baby.

"I'm sorry, Pippa. I daresay you meant well. But all I know is that you have given Judith a baby to care for, and that inevitably that baby will be taken away from her. And what will happen then, I just can't imagine. It nearly killed her last time. This time – maybe it will finish the job – "

And heavily, he turned and walked up the stairs, following Judith and leaving me to stand staring up at him, and Max and the little dead mother in the consulting room behind.

"Now what have we done, Dr Fenwick?"

Max's voice made me turn, and I saw him leaning against the consulting room door looking at me with that sardonic twist to his forehead.

"You've got an absolute gift for meddling, haven't you? You do a good job, medically speaking, and then go and ruin it by some absurd impulsive action like this last piece of stupidity. Well, what are you going to do *next*?"

CHAPTER SEVEN

I wouldn't have thought it possible that a person could disappear, in this day and age, and not be noticed. But that is just what happened to the young girl who had so unexpectedly appeared at Downlands, given birth to her baby and then died, in the space of an hour or so.

Of course we notified the police of her death and the baby's birth, and a coroner's inquest was held. The police tried to find out where she had come from, where she had been working, who her family were, but with no success at all. Inquiries at local factories showed that the turnover of staff was so rapid that no one could positively identify a girl who had left a week before. Inquiries at lodging houses, too, failed.

"Someone's holding on to her few things and saying nothing," Peter said two days after the girl's death. "It's not the first time it's happened, and it won't be the last, I daresay."

And so it seemed. Newspaper accounts failed to bring forward anyone who had known the pathetic dark-haired girl with the amber-coloured eyes, no parents, no boy-friend ("What was Emma's father like, I wonder?" Judith mused, looking down at the crumpled-rose-petal face of the baby sleeping in her arms) and we had to face the fact that no one ever would know. Emma's mother had disappeared like a stone thrown into a pond. But the existence of Emma herself was enough of a memorial.

She was an enchanting baby, and the effect she had on Judith was incredible. She seemed to shed years in the long hours she spent caring for the scrap of humanity that was Emma. All the pent-up love and maternal feeling of years came pouring out in a flood over the child, who thrived on it. She slept, and fed, and slept again. She lay blinking solemnly up at Judith's face as Judith dressed her lovingly in the beautiful baby clothes that had once belonged to her Emma. She lay beside the Coopers' bed in the beribboned bassinet that had also been kept from the past, and Judith would sit on her bed and just look at her as she slept.

On the day Charles was due to arrive for the weekend Peter called me into his consulting room just before morning surgery, and I went a little nervously. I knew the Children's Officer had come from the council the afternoon before, and I was afraid for Judith. Had I in fact done more harm than good in giving Judith the baby to care for? Were the local authority going to take Emma away to be put in a home?

"Pippa, I owe you an apology," Peter said abruptly.

He began to walk restlessly up and down, and I sat myself on the edge of his desk and waited. There was nothing I could say – yet.

"You were right. Judith *did* need a baby to look after. It's quite incredible the difference this has made to her. She hasn't taken a drink, or even seemed to think of taking one, ever since you put Emma into her arms. For the first time in years the ghost of our own child has been exorcized."

He stopped and went on with a rueful grin, "She's even helped me. She's a beguiling little wretch, and I'm getting decidedly attached to her, even in a couple of days. Anyway, the Children's Officer came yesterday and saw us – "

"I know," I said swiftly. "And I'm sorrier than I can say, Peter. If I'd stopped to think – which I suppose I don't do often enough – I'd have realized there'd be – problems – "

"But there aren't!" Peter said. "Not insurmountable ones, anyway. We were honest with Miss Lamont – Judith especially. She told her all about herself – about our own Emma's death, about her drinking, everything. We talked for – oh, ages. And then Miss Lamont said she felt she would be justified in leaving Emma with us for the time being – although we must face the risk that in due course we'll have to part with her. But she says there's nothing to stop us from making an adoption application – and as long as Emma thrives with us, and there are no – problems with Judith, there won't be any opposition to the application from *her* department. Of course the fact that I'm a doctor may have helped a little. Miss Lamont knows me well and knows I'll do all I can to keep Judith on an even keel. She also knows that having Emma may be all Judith needs to put her right again – for good."

He gave me a lopsided grin. "I'm deeply grateful to you, Pippa. And apologize humbly for being so – difficult the night Emma was born. You were right and I was wrong – because we've got at least a fifty-fifty chance of keeping Emma always. We're even registering her in our name – there's nothing to stop that being done since no one knows the name of either of her parents – "

I slid off the desk and ran across the room to put my hands on his shoulders.

"Oh, Peter, I'm so glad for you – so very glad! I do hope it all works out right for the three of you, indeed I do! In

81

a way, this takes some of the sting out of the tragedy of that girl's death – oh, Peter, I *do* wish you happy, you and Judith and Emma – "

He looked down at me with an odd look on his face, and then, before I knew what was happening, he had his arms round me and was holding me very close, and kissing me with a deep warmth and tenderness.

I was so startled that I couldn't do anything, neither pulling away from him nor responding. I just lay there in his arms.

There was a sound, a sharp sound, and it seemed to break the spell. Peter let me go, and I whirled trembling to stare round the room.

There was no one there, but the door handle was just returning to its normal position.

"Someone saw us – " I said stupidly. "Someone came in and saw us and then went away. Who – ?"

"I'm sorry, Pippa – my God, but I'm sorry! I don't know what possessed me!" Peter said shakily, and then moved away from me to the window to stand with his back to it as he talked. "It was just that – oh, I don't know. I was feeling such a mixture of emotions – gratitude, and hope, and pity for that dead girl, and regret for Judith's wasted years – and you looked so very young and pretty, and were so close – but I can't think what possessed me all the same – "

He put his hands to his face, and I saw they were shaking.

"I – you won't misunderstand, will you Pippa? I love my wife very dearly – very dearly indeed. In a way, that's why I kissed you. Can you comprehend that? It's because I love Judith that I kissed you. It sounds so stupid put like that – but it's true. Some men can love one woman and admire others – and that's the sort I am. But however much I admire a girl, there's still only one woman for me, and that's Judith – "

"Peter, Peter!" I said soothingly. "You don't have to explain, or apologize. I *do* understand, really I do. You needn't think I've got – designs on you! I'm truly happy for you and Judith. And anyway, I – I'm involved myself. There's Charles – the man who's coming down tonight – " and my heart lifted absurdly at the thought. "But what worries me is that someone came in and saw us. Who was it? And will whoever it was think there was more to an innocent kiss than a moment's indiscretion? We – it could cause a lot of trouble for us if it were the wrong person – "

I was thinking of Barbara Moon. She had already shown herself to be an emotionally unstable personality, suffering from an almost morbid sense of possessiveness about the men doctors in the practice. Look what she had done when she had merely *feared* I might come between her and them! What would she do if she saw what she would regard as concrete evidence? I was really worried.

And then, the door opened and Barbara herself came in, carrying a little pile of patients' cards.

"Several here for surgery already!" she said cheerfully and gave us both a limpid smile. "I've put some cards ready on your desk, Dr Fenwick. There are three new ones asking specially for you – you're getting very popular!" and with a gay nod she went out, closing the door behind her.

Could it have been Barbara who had seen us? Surely not! She would have to be a superb actress to appear so unconcerned so soon afterwards if it really had been her. And yet – didn't she put on a remarkable show of innocence when we talked together, all of us, about the damage to my medical bag?

"There's no point in worrying about who it was or wasn't," Peter said wearily. "If it's a mischief maker, we'll find out soon enough – and if not, well we were lucky. All I can say is I'm sorry – and it won't happen again."

"Forget it," I said, suddenly feeling as weary about it all as he was. "I'll start my surgery – and we'll just wait and see what happens."

It's wonderful how work can take the edge off any worry. My morning surgery was busy and interesting and by lunchtime the silly episode with Peter was so far in the back of my mind that I was able to have lunch with him and Judith without any embarrassment at all. That kiss *had* been no more than a momentary indiscretion, and gratefully I let the anxiety about who had seen us sink into the back of my mind.

Nothing had been said to Judith about it, that much was certain. She chattered cheerfully all through lunch, planning a shopping expedition to buy a new pram for Emma so that she could take her out for walks, and together we discussed the pros and cons of various makes.

And all afternoon, I found excitement welling up in me as I thought of Charles' imminent arrival. Since Peter was willing to take my afternoon calls for me, I had time to go and get my hair done at the best salon in Tetherdown, and then hurry back to take a long bath and dress myself in a leisurely way before spending a good half hour putting on a careful make-up.

And when I'd finished it wouldn't be too immodest to say that I looked pretty good. The hairdresser had done my hair in smooth sweeps that shone blue black in the light from my dressing-table lamp, and the new blue eye shadow I was using made the most of the colour of my eyes. I was

84

wearing my favourite dress – a sleek-fitting black one that flared suddenly at the hips and that was trimmed with a huge but demure white lace collar and floppy white lace cuffs. I wore it with white stockings and gay red shoes, and the total effect pleased me enormously.

But I was so eager to be ready in time that I was ready too soon. It would be a good hour yet before Charles would arrive, and I felt the excitement in me mount to fever pitch as I went out of my room to the big sitting-room that overlooked the garden.

The fire was burning, flickering its gentle light over the pale walls and the handsome Swedish furniture, and I collapsed into a big armchair and tried to relax. There was no one to talk to because Judith was closeted in her room – as was usual, now – with baby Emma. I had to fill in the time by myself.

And then I heard footsteps on the stairs, and the door opened and Jeremy's head appeared round the edge.

"Anyone home?" he called, and then as I sat up and he saw me he suddenly went very pink. It was a most disarming sight, making him more little-boy-like than ever, and I smiled warmly at him.

"Only me," I said cheerfully. "Will I do?"

"Oh – any time – I mean, yes, of course. That is – "

I laughed. "Come in anyway. How are you? And how's your father? Have you seen him lately?"

Jeremy came in and sat a little awkwardly on the edge of the chair opposite me.

"I've just come from the hospital and he's fine – much better, really. Getting very bad-tempered and that's always an excellent sign, Sister said. That's why I came in – I thought I'd tell Peter – I'd no idea I'd see you – "

"Sorry to disappoint you!" I said, a little wickedly

85

because I knew perfectly well what he meant – but he always blushed and stammered so charmingly that I couldn't resist teasing him.

"Oh, Phillipa, I didn't mean that!" he cried, and he looked and sounded so distressed that I put out a hand and touched his.

"I know, Jeremy – I was only teasing you a little. Look, now you *are* here, and you've delivered your good news, why not stay a while and talk to me? I'm on my own for a full hour – and I'd love some company – if you can spare the time."

"I'd love to," he said eagerly, and then, "do you mind if I sit on the hearthrug? It's so much more comfortable than a chair."

"Of course!" I said. "You can stretch out flat on the carpet if you like! Would you like some tea or something?"

He came and sat on the rug at my feet, leaning back so that his tousled fair head was resting against my chair.

"No thanks. All I want is to sit here and talk to you. It's the nicest suggestion I've heard all day."

"Good! Then what shall we talk about?"

I leaned back and relaxed, looking down at him, and thinking of David. It had been a full fortnight since he'd written to me, so at least I knew he wasn't in any financial pickle. I was his first port of call in storms of *that* sort. But he should have written to me, anyway, I thought a little crossly. I was his older sister, his only living relative. It would be nice if he made more of an effort to remember the fact. It should be he who was sitting here and talking, not this other boy. But if my own young brother couldn't be here it was pleasant to enjoy the company of someone young enough to remind me of him.

86

"– what do you think, Phillipa?" Jeremy twisted his head to look up at me.

I came to with a start. Jeremy had been talking and I hadn't heard a word he'd said. And I'd asked him to stay and talk to me.

"Forgive me, Jeremy," I said contritely. "I was suddenly miles away – what did you say?"

He was still sitting in that awkwardly twisted position, staring up at me, and he didn't respond to my question at first but just sat and stared at me.

"Jeremy?" I said, a little puzzled. "What did you say?"

"How can anyone have eyes as blue as yours?" he said, and his voice sounded oddly thick.

I put a hand up to my face, startled. "That's an odd thing to say – "

He moved then, scrambling to his knees and turning completely so that he was resting his hands on each side of me, on the arms of my chair, and staring intently into my face. I leaned back, a little embarrassed.

"Phillipa – you really are the most – the most wonderful – "

And then, to my amazement and – well, yes, horror – he leaned forwards and with an awkward fumbling movement tried to get hold of me, tried to kiss me.

I pulled away, turning my head so that his inexpert kiss landed somewhere in the region of my ear.

"Jeremy! Stop this, for heaven's sake!" I said, rather breathlessly. "What on earth's got into you?"

He held on to me, with his hard young hands gripping my shoulders, and said in a deeply urgent sort of way, "I love you, Pippa. I've loved you ever since Dad brought you to the College that day – I haven't been able to get you out of my mind, truly I haven't – and seeing you here now, like this – looking so marvellous – you're the most beautiful girl in the world, Pippa – well, it's just too much for me, and I had to – Pippa, dear, dear Pippa – will you marry me? Please, will you?"

And he looked so much like a small boy pleading for a new football, instead of like the ardent young lover he believed himself to be, that I was hard put to it not to laugh.

But of course I didn't. Calf love is nothing to laugh at.

And at eighteen Jeremy was very close to being a man, even though to me, at twenty-four, he seemed very young indeed. He certainly has the build of a man, I thought a little nervously, aware of his big body and strong hands as he loomed over me.

"Please, Jeremy, could you sit down again?" I said meekly. "I can't possibly talk to you while you keep me pinned down like this – "

"Oh, Pippa, I'm so sorry – do forgive me!" He was all repentance, and immediately sat back on his heels, and rested his hands in his lap, looking up at me eagerly.

"Jeremy," I said slowly, trying to frame my words as kindly as I could. "I can't tell you how – touched I am. It's a great – well, honour is the only word I can think of – to be asked to marry someone. But there are a lot of things to be taken into consideration – "

"Oh, there's nothing to *worry* about, Pippa! I mean, about money or anything. I've got the farm, and it brings in a very good income already – and when I'm managing it myself, it'll make lots more, I promise you, and you'll have everything you could possibly want – "

I had to laugh then, but very gently. "Dear Jeremy,

that's the least of the considerations as far as I'm concerned. I'm thinking of far more basic things. Like the fact I'm almost six years older than you are – "

"Oh, Pippa, what does that matter? I was afraid you'd say something like that, but honestly, it *just doesn't matter!* I'm not a baby, you know. I'm a grown man, however young I may seem. The way I feel about you – nothing could be more – more adult than that – " and he leaned forwards again as though to take hold of me.

"No, Jeremy," I said firmly, pushing him back on his heels. "No. And of course, you're right. If people love each other, age doesn't come into it, any more than finance does. But the really basic thing is that – and I don't want to hurt your feelings, Jeremy, truly I don't – the really important thing is that much as I like you as a person, I don't love you and I never could. And that's all there is to it."

There was a long silence. Jeremy looked up at me, his face suddenly white in the flickering firelight, and as I looked down at him my heart contracted a little. How would I feel if I were rejected as cruelly as that, offered no hope at all of having the love I wanted so desperately as this boy seemed to want mine? How would I behave?

The way Jeremy behaved startled me, and made me respect him, too, for it was very adult, very – sophisticated even.

He smiled, a crooked painful smile, but a smile for all that. Then he spoke in a rather hoarse voice.

"Fair enough. Better to know now than go on hopefully hanging my heart out to dry – only to get it thrown back in the end. Thank you for your – honesty, Pippa. May I go on calling you that? And may we go on being friends? I wouldn't want to lose sight of you altogether, even if you don't want me – or my farm." And he tried to smile even more widely and I could have wept for his courage.

"Of course we shall," I said softly. "Of course we shall. I promise to forget this ever happened – that you ever said anything at all. And then we can go on as we always have – "

"Pippa –" He leaned forwards and took my shoulders in his hands again. "Pippa. Just one thing. I've thought – oh, so often, I've thought about how much I've wanted to kiss you. Just once. Please, Pippa? To – remember what might have been? Something to hold on to whenever I have to face the fact you don't want me?"

I looked at him, at his smooth young face so close to mine and I thought – poor Jeremy. Lucky Jeremy too, because one day a girl will love you as much as you deserve, and then you'll know what love is really all about. Why not let him kiss me, just this once, as he asks? No harm – for it will mean nothing to me and please him.

And I smiled a little and put up my face and he dropped his head and let his hard young mouth brush mine. It was a sweet and tender kiss, brotherly, as far as I was concerned.

And then the overhead light snapped on, as someone came into the room, and I turned sharply, to look, feeling rather foolish. Max was standing at the door, and his face held its sardonic twist, a look that was becoming painfully familiar to me.

"Dear me!" he said dryly. "I seem to have interrupted an idyll. Do forgive me, both of you! I came to tell Dr Fenwick that her *dermatologist* is downstairs asking for her," and the scorn he put into the word dermatologist was slight, but there all the same.

"You'll have to take your place in the queue, won't

you, young Redmond? Hard luck!" and he turned and went.

I jumped to my feet, my face flaming with anger and chagrin for myself, and embarrassment on Jeremy's behalf. But he, oddly, didn't seem to mind. He had a look on his face that was surprisingly contented, and he smiled at me as I turned back to him and opened my mouth to speak.

"No, don't, Pippa. Don't say a word. I'm going now – I'll take the kitchen stairs, so as not to bump into your – friend. And I'll never say a word about this again, and I wish you oh, everything you wish yourself. And thank you."

And he bent his head and brushed my forehead with his lips, and then turned and went out through the door that led to the dining-room and thence to the kitchen, on his way to the back door.

And I turned and made my way to the main staircase of Downlands in a whirl of emotion. Twice in the same day I had been seen by someone in a different man's arms. Had it been the same someone? Had it been Max who had seen me with Peter? In a way I hoped so – for he cared so little about me as a person that he would do nothing about it. If it had been Barbara Moon, on the other hand, or even Judith who had seen me with Peter, what might happen because of it?

But I pushed these thoughts away. The important thing now was that Charles was waiting for me at the foot of the stairs, and I ran down them like a bird.

CHAPTER EIGHT

He was standing with his back to the fire, his long elegant legs in their slender black trousers braced widely, his hands in his pockets. He looked so superb, standing there with his head high as he surveyed the hall of Downlands, that I stood breathlessly at the top of the stairs, just looking down at him, taking in the sheer marvellousness of seeing him again, and feeling my heart give the old familiar lurch.

He raised his eyes and saw me, and without otherwise moving, let his lips spread into a wide smile.

"So, there you are, my dear! Such a charming house, this! I had no idea you were living in such delightful surroundings. A dour character in tweeds grunted at me to wait here for you and then disappeared" – he waved his hand vaguely in the direction of the stairs – "I suppose he told you?"

"Yes," I said, trying not to let my pleasure show too much. "That was Max Lester – one of the partners. It *is* good to see you, Charle – "

"And better still to see you," and he leaned across and kissed my forehead. And the way that made me feel, compared with how I'd felt when young Jeremy had done the same thing, beggars description.

"Country life would appear to suit you! You've a new colour in your cheeks – and you're a shade plumper –

but pleasantly so, I promise you. You were looking frail enough to snap over one's knee when you left town! We must try to keep that fresh look about you even after you come back to the metropolis!"

"Come back?" I laughed and led the way to a sofa. Charles came and sat beside me, and leaned back in his corner, looking quizzically at me. "It will be a long time before I do that, Charles! I told you – I'm staying here until young David qualifies – and after that, maybe – "

"Are you?" he said and laughed. "I'm thinking perhaps you may be back in town before you expected. I'm hoping so anyway. There – there is something I want to talk to you about – very much indeed. That's why I'm here, you know! Not just to breathe country air for a couple of days, but to talk to you – very seriously."

I turned my head and looked at him, and suddenly my breath came thickly in my throat, and my mouth went dry, and when I spoke I could hardly recognize my own voice, it seemed to come from such a distance away, and seemed so husky. But it must have sounded normal enough to Charles, for he didn't seem at all surprised by my reaction.

"Really, Charles?" was what I managed to say. "That sounds very mysterious – but interesting too. What is this – something?"

He chuckled. "A plan. A project. A new way of life for you! But I refuse – flatly refuse to talk about it here. We need surroundings even pleasanter than this, and I know just the place. Spotted it as I drove towards the town, made sure it was in the *Good Food Guide* – which it turned out to be – and booked a table. The Black Swan and Cygnet it shall be. Glorious twentieth-century food and wine in a sixteenth-century hostelry! What could possibly be nicer, hmm? Go and get your wrapper on, my child, and we'll away to a splendid dinner."

And with my head whirling, I ran quickly upstairs and collected my black cloth coat and red bag and gloves, before hurrying along the corridor to tell Judith that we would be dining out.

She was busy bathing Emma, and just smiled beautifully at me and told me to have fun before returning her attention to the wriggling pinkness on her lap.

"He *does* care for me, he does!" I whispered to my reflection in the mirror at the top of the stairs where I stopped to check on my hair before rejoining Charles. "That must be what he means about plans, and going back to town. Married to Charles – of all the things in the world I want, it's that – and that's what he is going to ask me to do!"

And then I turned and with a composure I was far from feeling went down to where Charles was waiting for me at the front door.

He handed me into his big grey car – a Jaguar – with an old-fashioned courtesy that made a wonderful change from the way the other men treated me – Peter's easy camaraderie, and Max's brusqueness – and I settled into its leather-upholstered comfort with a luxurious sigh.

"Makes a change from country rattle traps, hmm?" Charles said as he got in beside me, and started the engine purring. "I make no pretence of liking the simple life. For me, comfort plus is the order of the day. I enjoy money and the things it can provide and I maintain that people who don't say the same thing are liars or fools!" and he laughed.

And I had to agree with him. Sitting in the quiet comfort of the big car, as he manoeuvred it through Tetherdown's quiet streets, and out and beyond on to the bypass that led in turn to the country road where the Black Swan and Cygnet was situated, I revelled in it. I let myself imagine being Mrs Charles Griffiths, being rich and comfortable and elegant, and it was a beautiful dream.

We reached the little hotel with half an hour to spare before dinner, and as I checked my coat, I looked round approvingly. It was a lovely place, full of ancient oak beams and huge fireplaces where great logs of pine and applewood burned aromatically. The stone-flagged floors had soft rugs on them and there were deep comfortable armchairs about. Beyond the lobby I could see the dining-room, gleaming with lovingly polished wood, and glittering silver and china, and sparkling glass all arranged on the whitest of linen tablecloths. I sighed a sigh of pure bliss, and turned and smiled brilliantly at Charles.

"You really have a gift for living, Charles! I've been in this town some time now, and I didn't know this place was here! If the food is half as good as the atmosphere this evening will be heaven."

"I hope it will be in more ways than one," Charles said, smiling his rather mysterious smile. "I hope you'll make a decision this evening that will change your whole life – for the better."

He laughed aloud at the immediately eager look that I couldn't help letting show on my face.

"No, not yet – not yet. Patience! We'll dine, and then later, over our coffee, I'll talk about it. Now, what shall I order for you?"

"Oh – sherry please – not too dry," I stammered. And then, feeling the tell-tale flush in my cheeks said, "I must tidy myself – I'll join you in a moment – " and escaped to the door discreetly marked "Ladies".

95

I was sitting at the little dressing-table, tidying my hair and repowdering my face when I noticed a girl come into the room behind me. She looked vaguely familiar, and I dropped my chin. I didn't want to see anyone I knew, not tonight, here with Charles. And then I realized how absurd I was being, and lifted my head again.

It was Jennifer Farr, I remembered as I looked at her, a young patient of mine. She smiled when she saw me, an oddly constrained smile, and bobbed her head and then almost scuttled into the washroom section of the cloakroom.

Puzzled, I put on my lipstick, and tried to remember what I knew about Jennifer – but for the life of me I couldn't recall why she had been to see me in the surgery. I see so many patients it's almost impossible to remember details of all of them.

And then I shrugged, and decided to forget Jennifer. She had probably looked a little guilty – as she had – because she was out with a boy her mother wouldn't approve of, and feared I would carry tales. Forget it, since it's none of your concern, I mentally advised myself.

But it was odd how something about this girl niggled at the back of my mind as I made my way back to Charles in the hotel's lounge-cum-bar. There was something important about her, and I ought to remember it – but what was it?

And then I saw Charles, and dismissed the thoughts. The sight of him standing beside the bar, a slim stemmed glass in one hand, was enough to drive anything out of a girl's mind.

We were given a quiet table for two, in a corner, and it was ready for us with our first course when the head waiter led us to it, for Charles had already ordered the meal.

There were candles burning in tall silver sticks, and a bowl of miniature red roses in the middle, and in front of each place was set a bowl full of gleaming darkness embellished with lemon slices, with crisp hot toast nestling in a napkin beside it.

"Charles!" I said, gasping. "Caviare! This is wickedly extravagant, isn't it?"

"Not a bit of it!" Charles said heartily. "Not a bit of it. You eat it and enjoy it – waiter! The wine, please!"

And after the caviare we ate fillet steak beautifully garnished with tips of asparagus and crisp shoestring potatoes. And then Charles crooked an imperious finger at the waiter who came and fussed with bottles and little copper pans and a spirit stove beside us, while he made crepes suzette.

And as I ate the first bite of the delicate orange-flavoured pancakes with the filling of orange and sugar and liqueur I sighed in sheer bliss. We had demolished a bottle of a deliciously delicate wine between us, and the room seemed to dance with beauty and Charles to look more agonizingly handsome at each moment. I had never been happier in all my life.

And yet – all the time something niggled at the back of my mind. I could see Jennifer at the other side of the restaurant with her back to me. She was dining with three other people – all men who looked a great deal older than she was, and seemed to be eating and drinking a good deal. But why should seeing her like this make me feel uneasy, come between me and my own delicious meal and wonderful escort?

"What's bothering you, Phillipa?" Charles' voice cut across, and guiltily I dragged my eyes away from Jennifer's back, and looked at him.

"I'm sorry, Charles. It's just that – there's a patient of mine over there, and something's bothering me about her – something I can't put my finger on – "

He looked across the room, and then turned back to me.

"Conscientious girl! It's very encouraging to see it, but you really must remember you're off duty now! Anyway, if I have my way you won't be bothering your head about *these* patients much longer."

At this, my niggling anxiety about the young girl across the room disappeared, and I turned my full attention to Charles.

"Please, Charles – you've been saying things like that ever since you arrived in Tetherdown. Don't – don't you think you could tell me what you mean, now?" and how I managed to keep my voice light, to pretend I had no idea what he was going to say, I'll never know.

"Over coffee," he promised. And wouldn't say another word until we were sitting in the comfortable lounge again, on each side of a log fire that was burning with a gentle hissing and filling the air with the redolence of its smoke.

The waiter poured our coffee, and gave Charles a balloon glass with brandy, and gave me a thimble-sized glass of Benedictine, and left us.

Charles looked at me over the rim of his glass, and then put it down and leaned forwards.

"Phillipa – I've always liked you, you know that?"

I managed to nod.

"I – hoped you did," I said huskily.

"Always," he repeated. "And I liked working with you, back at the Royal. It – was almost a surprise to find how much I missed you, after you left. Oh, I worked with other junior house physicians, but none of them could hold a candle to you – and then you wrote, and I realized you were missing London a good deal – and missing me too, a little?"

I nodded wordlessly.

He leaned back with a pleased look on his face, and then went on, "And then, as I told you, I took this suite of rooms in Harley Street. There's a charming little flat at the top of the house, and it really is a pleasant life – except that – well, this is where you come in."

He leaned forwards again, and I sat very still, my untasted glass in my hand, staring at him over the edge of it while my heart thumped thickly in my chest.

"I want you, Phillipa. I need you. With you beside me, I know I could do splendidly – build the practice to something really worthwhile. But I can't do it alone. And when I thought about it, I knew you were the only person I could possibly ask. What do you think?"

I couldn't say a word. I just sat and looked at him.

"Of course, I couldn't offer you a full partnership at first – in fact, probably not for some years. It would be hard work for admittedly small return, though you could economize by using part of the house – the basement – that could be made into a pleasant bed-sitting room for you. Of course, I know it would mean you would have to leave your young brother to fend for himself, but I hope you'll think working for me more than makes up for it – "

My head whirled, and I felt physically sick. I couldn't believe it, but his voice went on, blandly enumerating the work that would be involved, talking about the amount of salary he could pay me – and even in my bemused state, I realized that there was far more work than money to justify it – while I tried to pull myself together.

Then, I interrupted him, in mid sentence.

"Charles! This is a *business* proposition you're making?"

"What else, my dear? What do you think of it?"

"But all this would be private practice? Wouldn't you work any more for the National Health Service?"

I couldn't really have cared less about the details of his plans, but I had to say something, anything, to hide from myself and from him the way I was feeling. I had been confidently expecting a proposal of marriage, and what I'd been offered was a sordid business transaction, designed to milk as much money as possible from gullible patients, money that Charles would keep to himself and not even offer in the form of a decent salary to his assistant.

"– life's too short for philanthropy," Charles was saying. "I for one am sick and tired of caring for grubby specimens of National Health humanity – I prefer the pleasanter types who use Harley Street, and I'd confidently hoped that you'd join me – you'd be an asset to such a practice, both medically and decoratively!"

He laughed suddenly, "My dear, I can imagine the more elderly gentlemen of the practice taking a positive delight in bringing their skin problems to so charming a practitioner! As much delight as the elderly ladies will take in me – " and he laughed fatly and drank some of his brandy.

I stood up, and stood swaying slightly as he peered up at me in surprise.

"I regret I won't be able to accept your invitation, Charles."

I spoke very clearly, the wine, and the Benedictine giving me a spurious courage I was far from feeling.

"On several grounds. I cannot leave my young brother to fend for himself, in order to look after rich old people in Harley Street. I certainly can't afford to work the way you propose for even less than I am earning now. And above all, you make me sick."

I took a deep breath, and looked at him through the tears that were gathering in my eyes, in spite of myself.

"I thought you – you liked me a little, as I – cared for you. As a person. Well, obviously you don't. You just see me as a potential ally in a money-making set-up. Well, no thank you. There's nothing more we can possibly have to say to each other."

And gathering the rags of my pride about me, I turned and fled for the ladies' room, blinded by my tears.

There was a small hubbub going on in there, and the women involved were standing with their backs to me, which gave me time to pull myself together and dry my eyes.

Then someone turned and saw me, and gasped, "It's – it is, isn't it? The doctor?"

"Yes," I said dully. "What's the matter?"

"I don't know – " the woman said. "Oh, I'm that glad you're here – and to think I recognized you – well, it was meant, wasn't it? It's this lass here. I think she's had too much to drink myself, but there's some that say she's ill. Now you're here we'll know for sure."

I shook my head to clear the muzziness in it, caused by the excellence of the meal I'd just had, and the way Charles had made me feel, and knelt on the floor beside the girl I could now see lying there, as the women who had been clustered round her made room for me.

It was Jennifer, and as I looked down at her, at her partly closed eyes, listened to her deep sighing breathing, and noticed the smell of her breath – it was like acetone, a pungent familiar odour – I remembered. I remembered what it was about Jennifer that was bothering me, had been bothering me ever since I'd seen her at the hotel.

"What happened?" I asked sharply. "Did she come in and say she had a pain in her middle? And was she sick?"

"Why, yes!" the cloakroom attendant said, pushing forwards.

"That's just what happened! I reckoned she'd made a pig of herself, had too much to eat and drink, especially drink so I didn't worry too much. These girls! But then she keeled over like this, and it don't seem like an ordinary faint, that it don't – "

"It isn't," I said crisply. "This is a diabetic coma."

For what I had remembered was that Jennifer had come to me with a list of symptoms that made me suspect diabetes. I had sent her to Fenbridge hospital for a blood test, and then waited for results. And now I recalled that the results had come in a few days earlier, and I'd asked Barbara Moon to write to Jennifer telling her to come and see me about the results of the tests – which showed conclusively that she *had* got diabetes. And she hadn't kept the appointment. That was why Jennifer had looked so guilty when she saw me this evening –

"We've got to get her to hospital fast," I said. "Can someone phone for an ambulance?"

There was a scuffing sound and one of the women disappeared, but then I had a better idea.

"No – quick – there's another doctor here tonight – in the bar. A tall – good-looking man – " It hurt even to say that much. "Tell him there's been an emergency, and – and Dr Fenwick wants him to take a patient into Fenbridge for her."

Another woman nodded and ran off, while I turned back to Jennifer to loosen her clothes and make her more comfortable. There was nothing more I could do, for what she needed was urgent hospital treatment.

The second of the women who had obeyed my instructions came back, and her face was white and stormy.

"Dr Fenwick!" she said. "Dr Fenwick! Did you say that man was a doctor?"

I nodded, surprised.

"Well, thank God he isn't mine. Because when I gave him your message he just said 'Tell Dr Fenwick that I haven't time to waste on her wretched country bumpkins, and to look after her own patients. I'm going back to London.' What do you think of that!"

"It doesn't matter," I said, flatly. "It doesn't matter." Charles had gone out of my life for ever, and all I could say was "It doesn't matter. It doesn't matter – " I felt dead inside.

And then there was a small hubbub at the door, and the other woman came back, bustling importantly.

"I couldn't get an ambulance, Doctor," she reported. "Seeing they're all out, on calls right now – we've only the three in Tetherdown, after all – "

"Oh, good lord!" I said, anxiously. "This girl's got to get to hospital fast – "

"Don't you fret!" the woman said. "I phoned Downlands, and explained, and that Dr Lester, he said he'd come with his car and take the girl to hospital. He says to hold on here – he's on his way."

On his way – Max Lester. He'd know that Charles and I had quarrelled, for he knew I'd gone out with him tonight – and my pride shrivelled as I thought about it. I wouldn't have minded so much if it were Peter who knew, friendly, easy going Peter, but the short-tempered Max – that was something else again.

103

I crouched by my patient, now breathing even more deeply, and in a deeper than ever state of coma, and wished I were dead. Everything was going wrong for me. If I'd remembered about Jennifer's blood tests as soon as I saw her, I could have warned her to go easy on food and especially on drink, for an excess of both had undoubtedly contributed to her condition now. If I hadn't been so light-headed about Charles, so bedazzled by his London elegance, I'd have seen through him long ago for what he was – a self-seeking piece of conceit – and not let myself be hurt by him.

And now Max was on his way, to see me in trouble yet again. Indeed and indeed the world seemed a miserable place at that moment.

CHAPTER NINE

I sat in the back of the car with Jennifer's head cradled in my lap, staring at Max's uncompromising back in the darkness. He'd said very little since arriving at the Black Swan and Cygnet. He'd come quietly into the ladies' room, looked briefly at Jennifer, and then with a curt nod at me had scooped the girl up into his arms and led the way out to the car. I had followed meekly, and since he had started the drive into Fenbridge he hadn't spoken at all.

"Do you know this girl?" I asked, somehow needing to break the silence.

"No. Should I?"

As briefly as I could, I explained what had happened, making no effort to slur over my own part in her collapse. I couldn't forget that it had been my own lapse of memory that had contributed to it. If only I had remembered those tests and the broken appointment –

"That's silly," Max broke in brusquely. "We're doctors, not little tin gods. People come to us with their symptoms, and we do our best to diagnose the illness and recommend treatment. After that, it's up to the patient. If they haven't the sense to do as they're advised to do for their own good, then we can't be blamed. To wallow in guilt the way you're doing is stupid."

"From your point of view, I'm always stupid!" I

snapped, stung into childishness. "I can't put a foot right as far as you're concerned – "

"Not at all," he said coolly. "You've done rather well tonight, on balance. You remembered what was necessary when it was necessary and made a fast diagnosis. If you'd treated this as a simple case of drunkenness – which it could have seemed – you wouldn't have been the first doctor to have made that mistake. You recognized dangerous illness when you saw it, and took the right steps to deal with it. What more do you want? A medal?"

And crushed, I sat silent for the rest of the journey. There seemed nothing else to say.

In the silence thoughts of Charles and what he had said came crowding back to torment me, stinging my eyes with unshed tears of – what?

Almost to my surprise I realized it wasn't rejected love that hurt me, but shattered pride. Oddly, the realization made me feel better. Pride recovers much more rapidly than a lacerated heart, I thought. Maybe I didn't care that much for Charles after all?

And then I thought of his tall elegant body and his handsome face, and my heart gave the old familiar lurch. Clearly, I wasn't going to recover overnight.

The small fuss at the hospital when we arrived drove all thoughts of my own problems away, and gratefully I turned all my attention to Jennifer and her treatment.

Preliminary blood tests confirmed my diagnosis, and within minutes, Jennifer was settled in the intensive care ward with a special nurse to care for her, and intravenous drips running. Max and I saw her once more when she was finally settled and then went to talk to the consultant in charge before leaving.

"I'll ring you in the morning to let you know how she

gets on," he promised. "With a bit of luck we'll get her on an even keel by then, and we can set about stabilizing her diabetes properly. She'll clearly need insulin, and I suspect some fairly heroic dieting. She's plump – and that almost certainly contributed to her condition." He turned to me, then.

"You did very well, Dr Fenwick, to spot the diagnosis so quickly, and to have the good sense not to try any treatment before bringing her in. Too often less experienced practitioners in this condition go off half-cocked and pump insulin into these patients before they come to hospital – and when that happens it's much harder to evaluate the situation. Well done."

And I blushed absurdly and stole a look at Max. But he showed no response at all.

We drove back to Tetherdown in silence, but it was a different sort of silence now. I was exhausted. It was now two in the morning, and I'd had a long day both from the work point of view, and the emotional one. Two men had kissed me unexpectedly, and the one I had wanted to kiss me had, metaphorically speaking, kicked me in the teeth. And the thought was so absurd that I giggled aloud a little hysterically.

Max looked at me briefly, and raised his eyebrows.

"I'm sorry," I said. "I was just – thinking about the day. And it struck me as funny. Not that I could explain why – "

"Jeremy? Is he the joke?"

"No!" I flashed, hot with embarrassment. "Certainly not! He – he's a sweet boy who let his imagination run away with him. Lots of boys his age get the notion they – they care for a woman older than themselves. There's no more to it than that. It's only calf love, and he'll get over it – but I wouldn't dream of laughing at him! That would be cruel – and I sincerely hope you'll have the – the courtesy to forget what you saw this afternoon! I can cope with your nasty sneers, but I don't see why Jeremy should have to put up with them."

"Nasty sneers? Me?" He sounded genuinely surprised. "Surely I never sneer?"

"It looks very like it from where I'm sitting," I retorted, and relapsed into a sulky silence that lasted all the way to Downlands.

After that night, life at Downlands slipped back into its quiet ways, as spring drifted into a warm sunlit summer, and the days stretched themselves and yawned through the long tranquil days of June and July.

Judith was ecstatically happy, and her happiness illuminated her, shearing years off her looks. She put on a little weight and that suited her enormously, and the softness of her looks was only matched by the softness of her mood. As far as I could tell she hadn't taken a drink since the night Emma was born.

Judith's new happiness in the baby seemed to communicate itself to the rest of us. Peter became much more relaxed and exchanged his previous hail-fellow-well-met ways for more mellow behaviour as Judith's own relaxation made his life so much more easy. He was still easy-going, helpful Peter, but so much *nicer* a person than he had been.

Jeremy, too, found new happiness that summer. The first time we met after that day when he had kissed me and blurted out his feelings was a little embarrassing, I can't deny. He had flushed a patchy brick red, and stammered a little, but I had smoothed things over with talk about his father, and the awkwardness passed.

Dr Redmond made superb progress, and left hospital for good a couple of weeks after Jeremy had proposed to me. He was all for coming back to work, but none of us would hear of such a thing, and Peter and Max together arranged for him to spend a long lazy summer, recuperating properly, at the house of a friend of theirs in Cornwall.

But what really made the difference to Jeremy was Barbara Moon. Quite how it happened, I don't know, though I suspected that Max had had something to do with it. According to Peter he had, one evening, presented Barbara with a pair of tickets to Fenbridge repertory theatre with the gruff suggestion that she get Jeremy to use the other one. Quite how Barbara felt about this I never knew, for I was quite sure at the time that she was in love with Max. But, obediently, she asked Jeremy.

And as the weeks pleated into months, the friendship between the two deepened and ripened, until we were all used to thinking of Jeremy and Barbara as a pair. We were all happy for them, for Barbara especially, for now she too seemed to relax, to become softer and happier, just as Peter and Judith were.

So, everyone at Downlands was happier – even Max, I think, for with Dr Redmond away he had to work harder than ever, both at running the practice and caring for patients, and he thrived on work. Everyone but me.

I tried to be rational and sensible about Charles, about the way my romantic dreams of him had been shattered and left in shards about my feet, but it was difficult. All I succeeded in doing was becoming harder, somehow, as I wrapped a protective veneer of not-caring around my hurt pride.

But at the same time, there was one area in which

my pride in myself was enhanced rather than damaged – and that was my work. As surgeries followed visiting rounds and clinic sessions at Fenbridge hospital followed surgeries I learned more and more about the intricacies of general practice, learned more and more about the art of diagnosis and the management of disease, and I positively revelled in it.

Sometimes when I looked back on my hospital days at the Royal, when I'd thought I knew so much, I marvelled at the naïve creature I'd been. Hospital work is all very well, I thought, but for real medicine, you can't beat general practice.

I said as much one evening to Max, at the end of surgery. I'd gone into his room to report on Jennifer who had come to see me. She had made an excellent recovery and was now very well stabilized, her diabetes under complete control, on daily insulin injections. She'd lost the weight that was so dangerous to her condition, and looked a much happier healthier girl than she had.

"She's to go to Fenbridge at three-monthly intervals," I told Max. "For the rest, I've got the consultant's letter here, and he's very happy to leave her in our care otherwise. That's one of the best things about general practice, isn't it? The way you get the chance to follow your patients through – really look after them properly, as whole people, instead of just medical cases."

Max looked up at me, his head framed in the nimbus of light from his desk lamp. It had darkened early this evening, for high summer, but there was thunder in the air, muttering away in the distance, and the sky was heavy and dark with unshed rain.

"Do you really feel that?"

"I wouldn't say it if I didn't."

"I thought you regarded general practice as an also-ran sort of occupation – the backwater of medicine."

"I did, once," I said honestly, wandering across the room to sit on the window seat, my back to the glowering sky outside. Thundery weather always makes me uneasy. "But I've learned better. I owe an apology for my original narrowmindedness. All right?"

He leaned back in his chair, and only his hands were left in the light. His face was shadowed, but I was aware of his eyes on me.

"Well, if apologies are the order of the day, I must be honest and admit I owe you one. So – I apologize."

The thunder growled softly, and I shivered a little, hunching my shoulders against the gloom outside.

"What for? I mean – I'm only too delighted to accept an apology, any time, as long as I know what it's in aid of!"

I kept my voice as light as possible, trying not to show the childish fear that was building up in me. It's shaming to admit it, as a grown woman and a doctor to boot, but thunderstorms terrify me.

"For misjudging you." His voice sounded gruff, but this time I recognized the genuine feeling in it, not assuming, as I usually did with him, that it was due to bad temper.

"I thought you were just a flibbertigibbet," he went on after a pause. "A silly empty-headed girl who'd got herself qualified by a fluke, and was going to kill time here at our expense. Most of the women doctors I've ever known have been – that sort. Self-centred. Well, I was wrong. You're a good doctor. A damn good doctor. The children in this practice – and their mothers – get much better care now than they did, because you really understand them and care about them as people. We – Peter and I – haven't got your touch in this area, and we're delighted you have – "

111

It was a good thing there was so little light in the room, for I knew my face was flaming scarlet with surprised pleasure. I was so embarrassed that I seized on the only thing he'd said that could make an argument.

"I'm glad you think I've done well," I said. "But I think you're dreadfully prejudiced about women doctors. They aren't all as bad as you paint them, by a long chalk, any more than all men doctors are perfect. I've known plenty who were superb doctors – women, I mean. And if you always talked to other women doctors as you – "

But before I could finish – perhaps mercifully, because I was about to spoil one of the few friendly conversations we'd ever had by being rather rude to him – there was a huge and vivid flash of lightning, and a clap of thunder that seemed to come from right over our heads. The rain seemed to burst from the grim dark sky and throw itself at the earth in a frenzy.

And I – I, for all the world like a frightened toddler, let out a shriek and hurled myself across the room in an agony of absurd terror.

It was so silly. I found myself clutching Max like a drowning person, my hands clinging to the tweed of his jacket as though it was all that stood between me and imminent death. My face was buried in his chest, and he was holding me and rocking me like the baby I was.

There was another clap of thunder, but further away this time and still I clung, unable to loosen my hold, unable to still the heavy terrified thumping of my pulses. But a third growl of thunder, now much further away, brought me back to my senses, and I let go, and pulled away, my body still trembling.

"I – I'm so sorry – " I said, putting up one shaking hand to tidy my ruffled hair. "I – it's stupid, I know, but there it is, I've always been scared of thunder – ever since I was a baby. Every time I think I've grown out of it, but one big clap, and I'm as bad as ever again."

He chuckled softly in the darkness, and spoke rather loudly to make himself heard above the drumming of the rain on the window panes.

"It's nothing to be ashamed of," he said. "Lots of people are scared of thunder, I used to be, years ago."

"You?" I peered at him in the dimness.

"Me," he said, and laughed again, but it was a gentle laugh, which warmed me. "And I found a way to cure myself. Come on." And he put a hand under my elbow, and propelled me, bemused, into the hall.

It seemed so odd, to stand there as he helped me into my coat, and put a scarf into my hand to tie over my head.

"What are we going to do?" I asked nervously as another clap of thunder reverberated through the house. The storm had turned, and was coming back towards us.

"You'll see," and his voice was kind and soft. "You'll see. Come on."

And he opened the front door, and beckoned me forwards.

I shrank back, terror rising in me again. Go out of doors, in a thunderstorm? I *couldn't*.

But he seemed to understand, and took my cold hand, and pulled me gently, and I found myself out in the pelting rain, as the huge drops bounced and splattered from the gravel path.

"Come on – " he said again. "That's right. Now. Stand here with me – you're safe, I promise you. Perfectly safe – perfectly safe – "

His voice had an oddly hypnotic quality, and obediently I moved forwards until we were standing side by side on the lawn, as the rain fell furiously out of the blackness above our heads.

He was still holding my hand, and after a moment he put both our hands in his coat pocket, and I shivered as the thunder muttered again, and shrank closer to him.

"Put your face up," he said. "Don't stand huddled like that. Put your face up, and let the rain wet it. It helps – you'll see."

And I did, somehow, in spite of my unwillingness, turning my face up to the sky above, but with fear still creeping icily in my veins.

It was extraordinary how comforting it was. The rain was warm but the drops stung my face agreeably, making me tingle, and as water dripped into my eyes and mouth, I suddenly giggled aloud. I couldn't help it. It seemed so stupid to stand in the pelting rain on a hot thundery night, getting soaked to the skin.

"That's better," he said approvingly, and then, "Now watch – watch for the lightning – it's beautiful, the forked kind – watch the sky – see – there? – wasn't that lovely?"

And it was. The vivid white spark, so huge and so magnificent, leapt across the heavy clouds like some mad ballet dancer, illuminating the tops of trees in a blinding flash of glory. And as I stood there with my head craned back, the imprint of the flash of light still clear in my eyes long after it had gone, the accompanying roar of thunder just went unheeded. I hardly even noticed it, so eagerly was I watching for the next flash of lightning.

How long it was we stood there, watching the lightning, my hand held warmly in his coat pocket, I'll never know. The lightning leapt and danced and it was as though I leapt and danced with it. The heavy warm rain ran down my face, and through my scarf to my hair – even to my scalp – and it felt marvellous.

And then, the rain stopped, gradually, and the garden stood steaming gently as the evening light returned. There was a heavy scent in the air, from the roses which drooped heavily on their dripping bushes, and the air was filled with the rich redolence of warm wet earth. And I sighed deeply and tremulously and turned my wet face up to Max.

"Thank you," I said simply. "Thank you. I wouldn't have thought it was possible to enjoy a thunderstorm – but I really enjoyed that – and I wasn't a bit frightened."

"You never will be again," he said softly, looking down at me, his face very close to mine. "That's a promise."

We stood there in the wet garden with the pale eggshell blue light of the sky that was appearing behind the scudding thunderclouds illuminating our faces, and I saw him as I never had before. A craggy face, yes, an experienced lined face, but not a hard or harsh one as I'd always thought. A kind face, really, I found myself thinking in wonderment. Now I know why the patients like him so much.

There was a sudden rustling sound, and then we both jumped as the white cat that lived in Dr Redmond's kitchen went skittering across the garden from her hiding place in the bushes, her fur spikily erect from the rain, an expression of outrage in every movement she made.

I suddenly felt a wave of acute embarrassment, and pulled away from him, and he let go my hand at once.

"I – I must look a sight," I said, foolishly, pushing a wet strand of hair from my forehead.

"No," he said gravely, his eyes still fixed on my face. "You look fine to me."

And then this mood seemed to change abruptly, and he spoke with his usual brusquerie.

"And now you'd better go and get yourself dry and change into warm clothes. You'll get a chill, and we can't afford to be one short at the moment, the practice is so busy."

"Yes, of course," I said. And turned to go.

At the front door I turned and looked back, to where he was still standing in the middle of the lawn.

"Thank you again," I called. And he inclined his head, just once, and I went in and squelched up the stairs to a much needed hot bath, my thoughts in a turmoil. This man, this maddening bad-tempered, gentle, cruel, kind, *paradoxical* man! Would I ever get to know him properly?

CHAPTER TEN

I would have thought that Max would have been friendlier after the way he'd helped me cope with my fear of the thunderstorm, but in his unpredictable way he seemed even more withdrawn than ever. Which was a pity, because I had begun to look at him in a new light.

I had begun to look at him as a person in his own right, instead of just as Dr Max Lester, the man I had fallen foul of from my very first day in Tetherdown. I began to wonder *why* he was the sort of man he was – why he was so short-tempered and brusque, what made him live so curiously withdrawn a life. For it was very solitary; as far as I knew he had no interests outside his work, no friends or private activity, apart from occasional fishing trips to the river which meandered through the fields just outside Tetherdown.

But I had no time to think much about Max Lester or anything else – not even to share the anxiety that crept into the lives of Peter and Judith as the day for the court hearing of their application to legally adopt Emma drew near. Because my own private life caught up with me again.

It was about a week after the day of the thunderstorm. I was finishing surgery, and curiously enough I was alone in the house again. Peter and Judith had taken Emma to visit Peter's sister and brother-in-law who lived in Surrey –

it was a Friday and they were away for the whole weekend – and Max was out on a visit. I'd let Barbara go early as she had a date with Jeremy (those two always made me feel so maternal, somehow! Whenever Barbara said she had a date with Jeremy I did all I could to let her get away in good time).

Anyway, I was just clearing up after the last patient, who had had a series of skin tests, when the doorbell pealed sharply. For one brief moment it was as though time had turned on its own heel, and it was again the night when Emma's mother had arrived out of the darkness. But then I shook myself, and went to answer the door a little wearily. Another late patient, I thought.

It was so late in the evening that the sun was setting, and when I opened the front door, which faced west, I was nearly blinded by the golden light that poured in to spill across the polished wooden floor and light the roses on the low coffee table in the centre of the hall with a vivid beauty.

I shaded my eyes with my hand, and said, "Who is it?" And then gasped as I was grasped in a huge hug, and swung round, my feet clear of the floor.

"David!" I cried. "David! How marvellous to see you! Where did you spring from, you young reprobate? Why – " and then my voice sharpened as I realized fully what this visit meant. "David! What are you doing here in the middle of term? Are you in trouble or something? Is it money?"

He laughed hugely, throwing back his head, and then said gaily, "Not a bit of it! Not money – well, not *directly*. No, Flip, my love – I got permission. Told the Dean I had to visit my poor sick sister, buried in the wilds of the country. I painted such a pathetic picture for him he waved me goodbye with tears in his eyes!" and again he hugged me.

As I extricated myself from his bearlike grip there was a movement behind him and I peered over his shoulder, surprised. There was a girl standing there, and I looked at her in amazement.

She was a mousy little thing, fair and pale, with long hair that straggled over her narrow shoulders. She looked vaguely unwell, I thought, as my professional eye took in the violet shadows under her eyes and the set of the mouth, a set that indicated underlying stress of some sort.

David looked over his shoulder to follow my glance, and then put his arm out to draw the girl into it, so that we were standing on each side of him.

"Flip, best of sisters, meet Fiona, best of girlfriends!"

The girl smiled at me with closed lips, a little warily I thought, and then spoke in a soft voice.

"Hello, Phillipa. I've heard a lot about you. I – I hope you don't mind us arriving out of the blue like this. I told David he should have phoned, at least, but he wouldn't – "

"I know David!" I said, and laughed, and held out my hand.

"Hello, Fiona. I'm delighted to meet you – though I can't pretend to have heard anything at all about you! This wretch hasn't mentioned a girlfriend in his letters – "

"I'm a wicked correspondent, aren't I, Flip?" David chuckled. Somehow there was a strain behind his laughter, and I looked at him sharply. I could see him more clearly now, for he had closed the door, and the blinding sunshine had gone, leaving the hall bathed in the clear light from the window. He looked strained too, I thought, and anxiety sharpened in me. This young brother of mine, part of my mind thought resignedly, this young brother, always in difficulties of some sort. What was it this time?

119

I put the thought into words. "Yes you *are* a shocking correspondent, wretch! The only time you write is when you need help – so I suppose this visit means even more urgent help is needed! I mean, it's lovely to meet Fiona, but I can't imagine you've come all this way just to be sociable!"

"He hasn't," Fiona said, and pulled away from him. "I – he – well, we need help. Badly. And David said you were the person to come to."

She stood there drooping, in the middle of the hall, and looking at her I felt my heart twist. She looked so pathetic in her gay with-it clothes, her long soft baby-fine hair spreading on her shoulders, and her air of frailty.

There was a long pause and then I said, "You'd better come in here," and led them into my consulting room. I felt obscurely that it would be easier to be firm with David in my professional setting. He was always able to twist me round his little finger, but this time I was determined to be firm with him. I just could not afford to go on dishing out cash as I had done.

As I led the way into my consulting room I did a rough mental calculation of what he had cost me the past six months or so, and realized it was well over fifty pounds in pocket money alone. No, it would have to stop.

So, my face was set as I turned to look at them. I stared very directly at David as I spoke.

"If it is money you need, as usual, David, I have to tell you right here and now that there just isn't any forthcoming. I don't want to be selfish or cramp your style any more than I must, but you'll just have to face the fact that you can't afford to spend as you do. I'm a working woman, and I don't earn all that much – and I've got to get some savings behind me if I'm ever to return to the career of my choice. I don't think I'm wrong to consider my own career to be at least as important as yours. Fair's fair, David. I'll do my best for you – I always will. But I won't be your financial doormat."

He began to prowl about the room, while Fiona sat silent on the chair near the door. David didn't look at either of us as he spoke.

"No, it's not money, Flip – that is, only indirectly. If I'd had any, I wouldn't have to come to you now, but I didn't, so here I am. But it's not money I'm going to ask you for. It's really something very simple – it won't cost you anything, nothing at all, really, so I'm sure – well, I'm *hoping* I'm sure – that you'll say you'll help us."

"It's no use talking in riddles David," I said sharply. "And of course I'll help you if I can – even financially, if it's really urgent help you need. I'm just making it clear I'm not handing over my hard-earned money for you to spend frivolously. That's all."

"Oh, there's nothing frivolous about this, Flip," he said and this time he turned and looked at me mournfully. "Promise you'll help, Flip? Promise?" and the familiar wheedling note in his voice made me feel so wicked, as though I had refused food to a starving child. But I hardened my voice.

"I've told you – I'll help if I can. But until I know what on earth it is that's bothering you, I can't promise anything – so *what* is the problem?"

He began to prowl again, and I sat on the edge of my desk and watched him, a worried crease between my brows. I'd never seen him quite so bothered before, not insouciant David who always managed to charm his way out of all his problems, who never seemed to care much

121

one way or the other – and got away with it time and again in consequence.

"It's hard to explain, really. Like, I don't know where to begin – "

"At the beginning," I said crisply.

"I'm trying!" and there was an uncharacteristic snap in his voice. "Like I said, it's a long story, and – "

Fiona's voice was low and husky and it cut across the room with all the clarity of a firebell.

"I'm pregnant," she said baldly.

There was a long silence as I sat and stared at her, and David stood frozen into immobility by the window.

"What?" I said stupidly.

"I'm pregnant. That's what David is trying to tell you. I'm pregnant and he's the father. It's as simple as that."

David looked at me, and raised his shoulders and eyebrows in a comical fashion that suddenly made me want to slap him, though in the past such tricks had always disarmed me completely.

"There you have it in a nutshell, Flip," he said. "I should have had more sense, I suppose. I mean, no one thinks the worse of people these days for having all the fun they want, but I was a nut of the first order to let Fiona cop a baby, wasn't I?"

"You're revolting," I said icily. "To talk so flippantly about something as important as a baby. Babies matter, David. You can't just talk your way out of this pickle, or charm your way out of it either. What do you propose to do about Fiona and your child?"

"Don't talk like that!" David said, moving sharply with an expression of distaste on his face. "You – you make it sound like a real person. And it's not – yet. It's just a problem to be solved. And that's where you come in – I hope. You won't regret it, Flip, I promise you."

He came over and stood in front of me, to take both my hands in his and look earnestly into my eyes.

"I promise you won't regret it, love. And no one but us would ever know anything about it – "

"About what?" I said, feeling stupid. I just couldn't catch hold of what he was trying to say.

"I don't see what – " I went on, and then Fiona cut in again.

"He's asking you to procure an abortion for me," she said clearly, and again a silence that was like a solid thing descended on us and we sat in that golden lit room in the light of a high summer sunset like frozen statues.

"I don't – I don't believe it," I said, and my voice sounded cracked in my own ears. "I just don't believe it. You're asking me to – look, David, you know my views of abortion. There are times when it's fully justified – and others when it isn't. This is *not* a case where any responsible practitioner would dream of recommending abortion, unless – "

I turned to Fiona.

"Fiona," and I spoke as gently as I could. "Fiona, are you a healthy person? Have you any diseases that you know of?"

She shook her head.

"Ever had any psychological problems? A nervous breakdown?"

Again that dumb negative.

I turned back to David, who was now standing with his hands dangling at his sides staring at Fiona with a baffled look on his young face.

"Then, David, I will not only refuse your highly

improper request – and I'm speaking now as a doctor, and not as your over-permissive big sister – I'll also forget you ever asked me."

I walked round my desk and sat down, pulling a piece of paper towards me.

"What is more to the point now is to make the right arrangements for your care, Fiona. Now – "

But suddenly Fiona was on her feet and staring at me, leaning over the desk, and leaning on her clenched fists.

"You won't?" and she spoke through gritted teeth.

"No, I won't," I said quietly. "I'm sorry, Fiona, but I couldn't. Not possibly. It wouldn't be right for you, it wouldn't be right for the baby and anyway – I couldn't bring myself to – to destroy a child who would be my own niece or nephew. I pity you very deeply, and I'll help you all I can – but not that way."

She whirled then, and stared at David, her head held in a challenging sort of way.

"And what about you, David? How do you feel now? I told you how I feel, but you – you didn't want to know. You're as bad as my parents, you know that? You've said enough about them, about their stuffy middle-class morality, but you're cut out of the same piece of cloth. Never mind how *I* felt. Never mind what *I* wanted. Never mind – never mind the way I loved you once. When it happened. Because, believe me, David Fenwick, I don't love you now, any more than you love me – any more than you ever did. You've only ever loved yourself, and I was bloody fool enough to delude myself into believing you could care for me, and could love me properly. You – you make me sick!"

I stood up then, and stared at both of them.

"Fiona! Are you trying to say – do you mean that your

parents want you to have an abortion too? *And that you don't want to?*"

She turned then and spoke softly, and very directly.

"That's just it. The first thing he said when I told him – " and she indicated the silent David with a toss of her head, "the first thing he said was 'how can we get rid of it?' Rid of it! I loved him – loved him enough to make love to him, and when I knew about the baby, I was glad, do you know that? I was *glad*. A love-child, I thought – a beautiful thing to be. A love-child. And then he – he said 'get rid of it'. I think that was when I started to hate him – "

David moved sharply then, his face twisted with pain, but she turned on him with such anger that he shrank back.

"Yes – hated *you!*" and she nearly spat the words at him. "I haven't said it to you before because you were too busy working out your own little sordid ideas to pay any attention to what I wanted, or how I was feeling. And then when my parents said the same thing, it seemed to me that – oh, I don't know. There was nothing else to do but go with the wind. So I let him bring me here. He swore you'd see us right – that was how he put it. You'd see us right, he said. And with so many people thinking it was the right thing to do – I don't know. I thought maybe I was crazy to want the baby, to want to stay pregnant and give birth to a child of my own."

Quite suddenly, she sat down again on the edge of my desk, and the colour that had filled her pale cheeks with a delicate peachlike flush faded and left her looking more washed out than ever.

I moved then to come round the table to sit beside her, but she jumped up and ran to the door.

"No – don't come near me, any of you. I know what's

going to happen – what always happens with David. He'll wheedle and cajole and persuade you to do it. And then you'll start on me, and you'll tell me, like my parents did, that I'm stupid to want to keep a baby, that it'll ruin my career, and that I'll never get my degree, and that it just isn't worth it, and I can have lots of babies later on if I want them – oh, I know how it'll be – and I want no part of it!"

"It won't be like that, I promise you, Fiona. I truly promise you. He won't cajole me this time. He can always get money out of me because that isn't all that important, but this time he'll find I can't be budged. It matters too much, you see. Far too much. You can trust me, Fiona. Let me look after you, please?"

But she shook her head, leaning there against the door, her pale face gleaming against the dark wood, for the room was rapidly getting darker now, as the sun finally disappeared behind the trees in the garden outside the window.

"No. It's too late now. A love-child means a child who is loved – not only one that's conceived in love. This baby, even if I have it, won't be a true love-child, because its own father will hate it and wish it had never been born, and so will its grandparents. So what's the use? I'll do as they want – your brother, and my parents. I'll do as they want, but I'll do it my way, with my own money."

She lifted her chin and looked at David then.

"You didn't know that, David, did you? That I had some money of my own, all tucked away safely, where you couldn't get at it? Well, I have, I – I was saving it for the baby."

Her voice cracked suddenly, and she took a deep breath before she went on.

"I was saving it to live on during the last months, when I couldn't manage to work anymore, because I was going to leave the University and take a job. And I was saving it for things like prams and nappies and sleeping suits – "

And now tears were streaming down her face, and I felt tears of sympathy in my own eyes as I looked at her, distraught as she was, and clearly not really able to think clearly.

"Anyway, I shan't want it any more for that. Because I'm going to find someone who will get rid of it for you – for you, not me, but for you, its father. Remember that. You're the father and you're making me kill it because you don't love me or the baby you made. That's what I'm going to do, all on my own, and I don't care what happens to me, or you or anyone – "

And then she moved with an incredible speed, and had wrenched the door open and run across the hall before we knew what had happened.

It was a moment before either of us came to properly, and then we were both running full tilt after her, out through the front door which she'd left swinging open, and out into the garden.

I saw her disappear round the corner of the drive, her long legs twinkling as she ran, and I pelted after her, with David just behind me.

"Fiona," I screamed. "Fiona – come back!"

We had reached the main road as I cried out her name, and she was half-way across it. It must have been the sound of my voice that did it, for she halted momentarily in her headlong run and turned her head to look over her shoulder, and then recovered her speed and ran on.

But not fast enough. Round the curve of the road I saw it coming as though in some slow-motion nightmare, a huge lumbering furniture lorry. I stood there, in what seemed like time held still, and saw the lorry moving inexorably towards her, saw her long legs moving with what seemed like interminable slowness, saw the big offside wing catch her and send her sprawling like a crumpled toy to lie beneath its wheels. And then I heard the high shriek of the brakes, the loud shouts of the driver, and saw a blur as David shot past me towards Fiona. And everything seemed to swing and lurch as the evening sky came swooping towards me, and the pavement came up to meet me in a blur.

CHAPTER ELEVEN

I think it was the shock of realizing that I had contributed so heavily to Fiona's accident that made me faint – something I'd never done in my life before. Certainly it was this realization that made me sit huddled, sick and miserable, over my desk long after Fiona had been taken to hospital in an ambulance with a pale and distraught David beside her.

For however I looked at it, the accident had been largely my fault. I had mishandled that interview so badly – so criminally badly. I should have remembered that a girl in the early days of a pregnancy, and an illegitimate pregnancy at that, is in a highly emotional state, liable to do anything. This poor child had been bombarded with advice to get rid of her baby, advice given by people she loved, none of whom seemed to realize she wanted the baby. And I, to whom she and my brother had turned for advice, had presented a rigid holier-than-thou sort of face that must have made her feel worse than ever.

And then, when she had gone careering off like that, I had shouted at her as she crossed the road – and as a result she was now in hospital, in heaven knew what sort of condition.

Quite suddenly, I couldn't stand it any longer. I had to know what was going on at Fenbridge hospital, what was likely to happen to Fiona – and to her baby. I'd had to stay at Downlands when David went off with the ambulance, because there was no one else to take emergency calls, since Max hadn't yet returned from his visit. But I couldn't sit there in the silent house waiting and wondering any longer.

I left a note for Max beside the phone, telling him I'd gone to Fenbridge to see about an accident case – there seemed no point in giving him further details. Then, I called the telephone exchange and asked the Supervisor to handle any calls that came through for Downlands.

"Certainly I will, doctor," she said cheerfully. "And if there seems to be anything really urgent, I'll call you at the hospital – drive carefully, now!"

And I did, because I had to. It was incredible how shaky I still felt, how much delayed reaction Fiona's accident had left in me. As I manoeuvred the car along the now dark roads through the warmth of the summer night, my thoughts chased each other round my head like a squirrel in a cage.

I seemed to have made such a mess of everything – my own career to start with. If I'd thought about it, there must have been some other way of getting over the financial problems created by Dad's death. And David – hadn't I spoiled him outrageously? Oh, of course it wasn't my fault the boy was quite as wild as he was – even in my self-accusatory mood I had more sense than to blame myself for intrinsic personality traits such as David's. But I hadn't helped him develop any sense of personal responsibility, dishing out money so freely, laughing so indulgently at his weaknesses.

And having made the decision for David's sake and come here to Tetherdown, look at the mess I'd made of *that*. Running afoul of Max Lester on the very first day, and never getting our relationship on an even keel – and it was clearly as much my fault as his that we hadn't got on. That night of the thunderstorm had shown me a different side to his character, had shown me that he was in fact a basically kind man. His patients loved him, his other colleagues respected him – it must be a fault in me that made us such bad friends.

And when I thought about it, there had been so many things I had done so wrong – the Higgins' case, the Jeremy episode, even the business with diabetic Jennifer – hadn't I mismanaged them all woefully badly? Really, I'd made an awful mess of everything. By the time I reached Fenbridge hospital I was in a very miserable frame of mind indeed, and it was only the effort of will that I used to avoid thinking about the disastrous business with Charles that stopped me from feeling positively suicidal.

I found Fiona still in the Casualty department when I had parked the car and gone hurrying on to the main block. David was sitting hunched unhappily on one of the benches in the waiting room, and he raised a tear-stained face to me as I came over and put my hand on his shoulder.

"Flip," he said huskily. "Hello, Flip. Are you all right now?"

And then his face crumpled, and he was crying for all the world like the little boy he had been so short a time ago, it seemed to me. I sat beside him and cradled his head in my arms and let him have his cry out as I stroked his shaking shoulders. A man who can cry, who isn't ashamed to let his natural emotion show, is lucky, and I knew better than to try to stop his tears.

He recovered fairly soon, and blew his nose vigorously, and dried his face before speaking again.

"I'll – I'll never forgive myself if anything happens to

131

Fiona," he said, and it was almost a whisper. "I didn't know how much she mattered to me, Flip, I just didn't know. I do love her, you know. In my own way, I love her very much."

"I'm glad," I said, and put out my hands to push his hair back from his forehead. "Loving someone is – important," and I tried not to think of my own loveless state.

"And it's not only Fiona," he said, staring over my shoulder into space, talking more to himself than to me. "It's the baby, too. I thought I didn't want it – thought the only thing that mattered was to get rid of it, but now – now I want it to be all right. So much. If – Fiona loses the baby, I shall – I don't know what I'll do – "

He looked at me then, his eyes re-focusing as he stared at me.

"It's odd, Flip – but it *is* a person – and more than a person. A part of me, of Fiona and me. No matter what happens, I'll never be able to forget that. We loved each other, and because of that there is another person. It's a marvellous, terrifying thought – Flip!" and suddenly his voice was agonized, and he clutched at me, and his eyes dilated with fear. "Flip! Tell me she'll be all right! Promise me she won't die – Flip? Promise me!"

And he sounded just as he had when he'd been small, and his pet mouse had escaped from the cage in which he so lovingly kept it. And I was just as helpless now as I had been then. I couldn't guarantee the mouse would come back, and I couldn't offer any reassurance about Fiona, for I didn't know yet what was happening.

I did the only thing I could do – opened my arms and let him creep into them for comfort. And after a while, as he sat huddled up to me he spoke again.

132

"Flip, can you forgive me? It was a lousy thing for me to have done."

"What was?" I asked gently.

"I was only thinking of myself, you see. Not of – of Fiona or you. It was bad enough to try to force Fiona into an – abortion, bad enough I wanted things to be solved that way. But to ask you to do it! My God, I must have been mad! You could have wrecked your career if you'd done it, couldn't you?"

"No – not really. Not today. The law is easier than it was, and if I'd felt it best for Fiona and the baby to abort her, I could have arranged it legally. But I didn't think it was best. In fact, I don't believe I thought at all," I finished bitterly.

"Don't blame yourself, Flip," David sat up and looked at me very earnestly. "You mustn't. You were absolutely right to say what you did, and you mustn't blame yourself – "

Across the waiting room, a door swung open, and a trolley with a nurse propelling one end and a porter the other, came through on silent rubber wheels. The nurse was holding aloft a bottle of ruby red blood, which was connected to the still figure on the trolley by a length of translucent tubing.

We both jumped up, and as the trolley went smoothly across towards the lift, a doctor came out too, and walked over to us. It was Dr Jefferson, a man I knew slightly from my clinic sessions at the hospital.

"Hello, Dr Fenwick!" he said cordially. "Now, this girl er – Fiona Matheson – is she your patient?"

"Well, not exactly. I mean, in a way," I floundered and he raised his eyebrows.

"I'm more of a relative," I said. "That is, this is David Fenwick, my brother – Fiona is his girlfriend."

"I see," he said, and looked very levelly at David. "Then – look, Dr Fenwick, I think I'll talk to you on your own, if you don't mind, and then you can talk to your brother afterwards – " and he took my elbow and propelled me across the waiting room to his small consulting room.

I looked back at David, and my heart turned over for him. He looked so anxious and bereft, standing there alone. But he looked older too, and I realized in that one fleeting moment that whatever happened, David wasn't a feckless boy any more. This whole sorry business had brought him face to face with himself and his own attitudes, and I could only pray that what he saw would make a true man of him.

Dr Jefferson sat me at his desk, and offered me a cigarette, but I shook my head.

"Well? What's her prognosis? How will she do?" I asked directly.

"*She* will," he said. "She'll be all right. She's concussed, but there's no skull fracture. And she's got a fractured pelvis that'll take time to put right. But she'll be fine in herself. However, there is something else – "

"The pregnancy," I said.

"You knew about that?" He looked relieved. "I was afraid you didn't. It could complicate things, since I gather they're not married."

"They're both still at University," I said. "But I know about the pregnancy. They – told me tonight."

"Knew," he said gently. "Past tense, Dr Fenwick. She aborted just after getting here. We're taking her to theatre now, to make sure all is complete. I'm sorry about it – though maybe it's all for the best, under the circumstances."

I shook my head. "It would have been – a few hours ago.

134

But now, I'm not so sure. She wanted it, you see. And my brother too – since the accident he's had a chance to think, and he's realized just what it meant. Poor babies." And I whispered it. "Poor babies."

"You'd better go and talk to him," Dr Jefferson said. "He'll need you for a while, I imagine. He can see her soon – she should be back from theatre and round from her anaesthetic in an hour or so – and then she'll need *him*. I'm sorry you're having so much family bother, my dear. Being a doctor isn't as much help as people think, when illness and trouble hit your own people, is it?"

And I agreed wholeheartedly, and thanked him, and went back to David in the waiting room.

The next hour was misery. It took a long time for David really to understand what had happened, but when he had, he sat there beside me, leaning forwards with his elbows on his knees, interminably turning his gloves in his hands.

"Fiona's all right," he kept repeating. "She's all right. And if she can forgive me, I'll make it up to her, somehow. We'll get married, won't we? Yes, we must. And we'll get by, and one day we'll have babies. We'll never forget this one but we will try again, and I can only pray it will be all right for us – tomorrow, or the day after tomorrow – "

And I sat beside him, and murmured the most encouraging words I could, while David sat and grappled with his own failings, his own problems, and made a huge and painful step towards the true maturity he had always lacked.

About fifteen minutes before we could expect Fiona to be ready to see us, there was a small scurry of activity in the waiting room, and several patients came in. I looked up, only vaguely interested, so involved was I with my own problems, and surprised, saw Mrs Higgins and her baby. It was odd seeing her again, for ever since the night I had first seen them, I had practically forgotten the whole episode. Seeing her again made me wonder what was going on with her, and what had happened to her husband, for I'd heard no more about him either.

David had fallen into a shallow exhausted doze, and on an impulse I got up, and went across the now busy waiting room towards Mrs Higgins. But as I moved past the crowded benches she turned – not having seen me – and went out again, the baby cradled in her arms.

I followed her, and stood for a moment on the dark courtyard outside the entrance, straining my eyes, but she seemed to have melted into the shadows. And then I saw a movement, and heard footsteps moving away, and I shrugged and turned back to the brightly lit Casualty waiting room. She must have gone, I thought.

But she hadn't, for as I made my way back towards David, I heard her come in behind me, and turned back to her with as friendly a smile as I could manage.

"Hello, Mrs Higgins! How are you? I haven't seen you for a long time. How's Gary?"

"Er – he's fine, thanks," she said, and looked at me, and then let her glance slide away. "Fine – I just came up to get some more of his special medicine. I broke the bottle at his last feed, so I had to get some more – I'll just pick it up, and be on my way – "

She seemed anxious to get away from me, but I persisted. I really wanted to know what was happening with her.

"Have – have you heard from your husband?" I asked as gently as I could. "Since – since he – er – left the hospital?" I could hardly say "ran away", I felt.

"No!" She said it so violently that I jumped, and that made her speak more softly. "No – I haven't. I've no idea

136

where he is. I hope he's – I hope he's OK, because for all his faults he's my man, and he can't help being the way he is – he's ill, see? That's why he goes on like he does. He can't help hating women doctors, after what he's been through, one way or another. You can't blame him for the way he was that night – "

"I don't," I said. "Of course I don't! I realize he's ill. That's why I wish he'd come back to hospital and get the care he needs, instead of hiding away like this. He needs help – and the sooner he comes back to us and gets it, the sooner you can all be happy together again. If you do see him – "

And I spoke very deliberately, for I was sure, from her nervous manner, and the violence of the way she had denied seeing him during the past months, that she knew exactly where he was.

"If you do see him, or hear from him, try to get him to come for treatment. I promise I won't be part of it – he can see Dr Lester, and Dr Lester will make sure to send him to a man specialist, I'm certain – and everyone will be on his side. I am – we all are, really we are – "

She looked at me very intently, shifting the baby from one arm to the other, and opened her mouth to speak, but just then a nurse came across to me.

"Dr Fenwick?" she said. "You can see Miss Matheson, now, if you'll come with me – "

Immediately, all thoughts of the Higgins family and their problems evaporated, and with a swift smile and a pat on the shoulder I turned away from Mrs Higgins, and went across to rouse David.

Together we went into the lift, and up to the ward, and I held David's hand very tightly as we went, for he was pale and sweating with anxiety.

The nurse took us to a single-bedded side ward, alongside the gynaecological ward, and I walked in in front of David.

Fiona was lying flat, her face almost as pale as the pillow against which she was lying. She was staring up at the bottle of blood dangling from a stand at the head of the bed, but she turned her head as I stood beside her, and looked at me.

"Hello, Phillipa," she whispered. "You've heard, I suppose? I – won't have to bother you any more."

My eyes filled with tears. She looked so very young and frail lying there, and I hated myself for letting this happen to her.

"I'm sorry," I said simply. "I – I'm truly sorry, Fiona. I wish with all my heart it hadn't happened."

She raised her eyebrows in an oddly dismissive sort of way.

"No point in apologies, is there?" and then she managed a smile, a weak smile that almost broke my heart. "I guess it just wasn't meant, hmm?"

And then her face changed, as her eyes moved so that she was staring over my shoulder. David was standing there, his face ghastly as he looked down at her.

For one brief moment, I thought she was going to turn her head away from him, and refuse to look at him, but then David spoke – and said the only thing that could have made Fiona even consider speaking to him.

"I love you, Fiona. Very much. I thought you were going to die, and I wanted to die too. Tell me you still love me – "

I stepped back, slipped away, leaving them to stare at each other. I had no place in this room any more, no place at all. These two would have to sort things out for themselves, have to come to terms with their feelings for each other, learn to face the tragedy in their lives in their own way. They had somehow to find a way through the unhappiness of the past weeks, find a new strength in each other.

The last thing I saw as I closed the door gently behind me was Fiona's hand as she lifted it from the bed, and David's as he reached down and took it in both of his.

"They'll be all right," I whispered to the closed door. "They'll be just fine – " and moved wearily away towards the lift to go back to Casualty and wait there for David.

But when I got there, the clerk at the reception desk beckoned me over.

"There's a call for you, Dr Fenwick, from the telephone exchange. You can call them back from here, if you like – " and she indicated the telephone beside her.

The telephone supervisor sounded very self-important as she delivered her message, and I listened to her thin voice come clacking from the earpiece with a sinking heart. I was desperately tired and the thought of coping with work right now made me feel even more exhausted.

"Langham's Farm, Doctor. Do you know it? About three miles along the lane that runs off the main road to Besterrick. It's a bit of a rough road but there hasn't been much rain lately so you should get through all right."

"What's the trouble there?"

"Ooh, I've no idea," she said. "There was this man who called – I picked up the call here of course, and he just said to ask Dr Fenwick to come right away, it was urgent, there'd been an accident."

"He asked for me by name?" I said, puzzled. "How odd – "

"I suppose he knows you," the girl said. "I never thought to ask his name – "

"Oh, well, I'd better get going, I suppose," I said wearily, "if it's as urgent as that. Take any further calls that come in, will you? Dr Lester should get back to Downlands fairly soon – and then you can give him any further calls that come in – "

"He won't," the girl interrupted. "He called in just after you, said he'd been back to Downlands but had to go out again on a maternity call, and didn't know when he'd be back. He said to ask you, when you called in, to hold the fort – "

I groaned. "That's all I needed tonight. I'm dead on my feet, and I've got to hold the practice on my own! Oh, well, can't be helped – "

I left a message for David with the casualty clerk, telling him to take a taxi back to Downlands, and that I'd find him a bed for the night when I got back.

Though what time that will be, I thought, as I made my weary way out to the car, and started the engine, heaven only knows. It was already close on ten and there was still this emergency call to deal with, some nine miles out into the country, and anything else that might come in in the next few hours. And experience told me that when one person was on call for the whole practice, it was odds on that there would be a rush of work.

I sighed, and shook myself, and then slipped the car into gear and swung out into the main road. The sooner I got there, I told myself philosophically, the sooner I'd get back to Downlands. And I settled down to the long drive to Langham's Farm.

CHAPTER TWELVE

I felt curiously unreal as the car sped through the dark leafy lanes, changing gear and turning corners, feeling the car pull as it climbed steadily, without really being aware of being at the controls. I was quite desperately tired, and when I remember I had done a very full day's work, a day that had culminated in the highly emotional time I had spent with Fiona and David, it wasn't really surprising.

The road levelled out, curved gently westwards, and I turned the headlights to full beam and peered through the windscreen to see if I could spot the opening to the narrow road that led to Langham's Farm. It couldn't be far now –

A rabbit ran across the road, almost under my wheels, and I swerved – and the sweep of the light showed the mouth of the lane I was looking for, almost hidden by overhanging leaves. I turned into it, and felt the engine complain as the wheels hit the very rough surface.

It was a deeply rutted road, with widely scored peaks of dried mud that from time to time hit the underside of the car with a violence that made my whole body shudder, and as the car bucketed and rocked along, I cursed softly. Why couldn't the farmer invest in a little macadamming for his road? I thought resentfully. Driving in these conditions is absolute hell. I hoped very sincerely that the patient, whoever she or he might be, wouldn't need to be transported back along it. It was rough travelling for the fit, let alone the injured –

And then I saw it. Far ahead of me, twinkling with a fitful gleam, was a light. A torch, or a lantern, I diagnosed, being waved by someone who was obviously waiting for me.

I couldn't see anything apart from a hulking blackness, only marginally blacker than the sky beyond, when I reached the light which was in fact a bull's-eye lantern being slowly waved from side to side.

Gratefully, I stopped the car, and sat for a brief moment as the silence of the summer night washed over me. But then I moved, swung my legs out of the car, and with my surgical bag in one hand peered at the dark shape in front of me.

"Hello!" I called. "This is Dr Fenwick – you're waiting for me?"

"That's right – "

The voice was low, almost a whisper, and I had to strain my ears to hear it. The figure moved backwards, and then the voice came again.

"This way – they're waiting for you over this way – "

I moved forwards gingerly, trying to see where to put my feet on the treacherous road, and said a little irritably, "Shine that light this way, will you? I can't see a thing. I won't be much use if I fall and break my neck – "

Obediently, the light moved, and came and lit the ground in front of me, and I moved forwards carefully, following the jerk of the light as my guide led the way.

The way the light led was off the road, and I paused as I found myself stepping over a narrow ditch into what seemed to be a patch of woodland.

"Where on earth are we going?" I called. "I thought the accident had happened at Langham's Farm?"

"It's up at the quarry," the husky whisper came. "Through here – across the copse. Not far. Follow the light."

And the light moved away, and I was forced to follow it, but not feeling very happy about it all. If there had been a severe accident at a quarry, heaven knew what state I'd find the patient in. They should have explained more about it when they phoned, I thought angrily. Then I could have laid on a rescue team of some sort.

"Why didn't you say when you phoned that it was at a quarry?" I called after my leader. "I may not be able to do much to help if the accident is a bad one."

"Oh, you'll be able to help all right – "

The voice was louder now, coming back to me through the heavy twisted trees, and for a moment I thought – "I know that voice – " But then I tripped and almost fell headlong, and swore under my breath as I felt my stockings tear against the rough bark of an outstretched branch.

I had just about decided to quit, to turn back to the road and go back to Fenbridge to call out a rescue team, when the darkness thinned a little and I could see the sky, a thinner greyer blackness above the trees.

We had reached a little clearing of some sort, I realized, for I could just see, now that my eyes were fully accustomed to the darkness, the trees start again a few yards away. But between those trees and me was a huge yawning blackness, and I knew we had reached the quarry.

"Well?" I called, my voice sharpened by nervousness, for I was undoubtedly bothered by the darkness and the silence broken only by the sounds of my own breathing, and the crack of the footsteps ahead of me. "Well? Where's the patient? What happened here? He was surely not left alone, was he?"

"Over here," came the voice, a husky whisper again, and the light swung invitingly.

I moved carefully, trying to see where I was putting my feet, and then my wrist was grabbed and held in a firm clasp.

"Over here," the voice said again. "He's down here. Hold on – I'll help you down – "

And I found myself moving down a narrow twisting path, covered with needle-sharp flints and pebbles that made my feet slide terrifyingly, for the path ran at an incredibly steep angle. I could feel rather than see the huge yawning gap before my feet where the quarry plunged away heaven knew how many hundreds of feet, and even in the darkness the thought made my head spin.

"Step to your right," the voice above me commanded sharply, and obediently, I did, and found my feet on a narrow flat ledge. The hand holding my wrist from above let go, and a few pebbles slithered on the path as my guide clambered up the path.

"Hey!" I called protestingly. "Where are you going? Is this the place? Where's the patient?"

The voice came from directly above me now. "There isn't any patient, *Doctor*. And the only one there will be is you, because that's the only way you'll ever be stopped from your busy bodying ways – "

I peered upwards into the darkness, trying desperately to see the face of the man above me, but then I shrank back as something heavy slithered over the top edge of the quarry, and with a heavy roaring lurch went careering down the sloping path beside me.

It was a lump of heavy rock, and as it went, the path seemed to fold up under its weight, sending a shower of flints and pebbles and lumps of the earth that underlay them rattling deep into the quarry. I heard the distant clunk and clatter as the rock and pebbles landed far beneath me, and shivered in sick terror as I realized just how far below me it was.

I moved a little sideways, trying to find the path again, meaning to climb back up it, somehow. And then realized that the path had gone, that the rock that had been pushed down it effectively had destroyed what little surface it had.

There was a peal of laughter above me, and I strained my head upwards, but all I could see was the dark shape of the head silhouetted against the sky.

"Who are you?" I cried. "You must be out of your mind! What sort of silly game do you think you're playing? For heaven's sake stop being so stupid, and pull me up, and we'll say no more about it – "

The man laughed again, and the light swung, as he pulled it forwards. I heard the scrape of metal as the shutter moved, and then the light suddenly splashed wide, and was directed upwards, so that it lit the face of the man who was holding it.

I don't think I was really surprised. I think I had suspected, ever since I had heard the voice more clearly back in the woods, the identity of the man who was sharing the darkness with me.

It was Higgins, peering down at me above the light, and laughing again as he stared at my face.

He stopped laughing then, quite suddenly, and begun to talk in an almost conversational tone.

"You've always been fond of busy-bodying, have you? Or is it something you just do to those that hate it most – people like me?"

"Please, let me get up," I pleaded. "I won't do anything

about this – won't tell anyone, I promise, if you'll just help me up – "

"Or is it something all you bloody women doctors do? Bad enough you set yourself up to do men's jobs – you have to go and meddle in what's none of your concern, shutting up better people than you are, and interfering with their wives and kids – "

"Look!" I cried desperately. "I've no wish to interfere with you in the least – you're Dr Lester's patient, not mine! I've had nothing to do with you or your wife or your baby for months! There was just that one time, when your wife sent for me – and I knew nothing about what was going on! Now, look, please, be sensible. Help me up, and you have my word I'll never meddle, as you call it, again. But this is crazy, shoving me down here – "

"Nothing to do with them? Nothing to do with them?" His voice was suddenly high and shrill. "So you're a liar too! I saw you, you know, saw you tonight up at the hospital there, meddling again, talking to my wife! I saw you – so don't tell me any more of your lies! I made up my mind right then, I did, made up my mind I'd put a stop to it once and for all! If I get you shut up for good then I'll go home and no one else'll ever meddle with me again. Do you know what? All because of you, and the way you got me locked up in the hospital again, all because of you I've had to live up here at the quarry like some bloody animal! I got out of that hospital, I did – there's no hospital'll hold me no matter how many busy-bodying women try – and here I've been ever since. And I'm sick of it, do you hear me? Sick and tired – so when I saw you down there at the hospital tonight, the first chance I've had to see my wife in all these months, when I saw you, meddling away again, I made up my mind. It's going to stop, do you hear me?

146

I've had enough and so has everyone else. You've had your knife into me all this time, and I won't stand it any longer – and now no one else'll have to put up with you either – "

"What are you going to do?" I cried, my voice sharp with fear. "What are you going to do –?" and fear rose in me in a great sick wave, making me sway a little on my narrow ledge, so that I had to cling desperately to the rough side of the quarry wall.

"Do? Nothing – nothing at all – " And he laughed again.

"I'm just going to go away, that's all. And they'll look for you, I daresay, but they'll not find you – not till you've fallen off that there ledge and landed all twisted and dead on the bottom – and they'll say – stupid bloody woman, meddling in what didn't concern her – serves her right, that's what they'll say – "

And then the light disappeared, and there was a scrabbling sound above me. A few pebbles hurtled past my ears, and I shrank against the cold rough wall in terror.

He was going away. This half-demented, pathetic, twisted creature was going away and leaving me here in the darkness on a ledge so narrow I could only stand on it, leaving me to die.

I screamed as loudly as I could, and the sound came echoing back out of the quarry with a curiously mocking note in it –

And when the echoes had died away all I could hear was the faint crack and rustle of the woods, and the hiss of a small wind that had sprung up in the distant trees, and I felt despair fall over me like a great sick blanket.

I'll never be able to explain how I felt, hanging there like a fly against the wall, or even how long the hell of it went on. Thoughts chased themselves around my head with sick monotony. I thought of David and Fiona. Of the long happy days so long ago at the Royal. Of Dad and the way he had looked when he gave me my surgical bag, and absurd things like the Christmases I had known in my childhood, when my mother was alive, and school, and University dances –

And, oddly, about Higgins. I felt no hate for him, no anger. The doctor in me must be strong, I thought wryly, awkwardly moving my numb feet, and shivering again as a few dislodged stones moved beneath my feet and then went tumbling deep into the quarry. I just feel desperately sorry for him, the poor sick creature. Even found myself hoping that somehow someone would persuade him to get the treatment he so needed, hoping that one day he'd be well again –

I hadn't even realized I was crying until I heard it, and the distant sound made me catch my breath, made the sobs stop in my chest, and I lifted my head and listened, pouring all the concentration into my ears.

And heard it again. A shout. A human shout, far away, but then repeated, nearer, and then again –

I think I must have screamed, and gone on screaming, for suddenly there was a light and sound above me, and a deep voice said, "Stop that – " and bemused, I closed my mouth, and heard the screaming that I hadn't realized I was making die away.

"Don't move. Just stand perfectly still and do nothing," the voice said sharply, and I rested my cheek against the wall between my hands, and obediently stood still.

There was rope, I think, and strong hands, and then I felt my body pulled protestingly upwards, and my hands and face scraped against the stone walls, and I whimpered like a baby –

148

And then, I was lying on my back on firm level ground, staring up with dazzled eyes into bright lights, aware of voices around me, and people, human bodies. And I closed my eyes again, and let the terror and anguish that had been so pent up in me well up, and I wept bitterly, feeling the hot tears under my lids and stinging my painful scratched and bleeding cheeks bitterly, feeling the hot tears under my lids and stinging my painful scratched and bleeding cheeks.

"Don't – oh, darling, don't – " The same deep voice spoke again, the voice that had told me to keep still, to stop screaming, and then I felt myself lifted in strong arms, and felt my cheek held close against another one, a warm rough cheek.

I put up one hand, wonderingly, to touch the face so close to mine, and felt it wet with tears.

"What?" I mumbled stupidly. "What?"

"It's all right now, my love. All right. You're safe now, and you'll always be safe – don't cry, my darling – don't cry – "

And as though I had been waiting for this moment all my life, I sighed deeply, and put my head down on Max's shoulder, and closed my eyes, and let my body go limp as he carried me away from the edge of that hateful quarry, back to life and safety.

I sat in the long low lounging chair on the terrace of Downlands, my bandaged hands resting on my lap, feeling the sun warm against my face, and lazily watching Judith and Emma on the lawn under the big copper beech tree. Judith had spread a rug, and was trying to teach the baby to crawl, but she just lay and blinked owlishly up at Judith and grinned her wide toothless smile, and waved her fat arms about, clearly not a bit interested in locomotion while she had an adoring mother to play with her.

For now Judith was her mother, really her mother. The news of the success of their adoption application had arrived in the post on Saturday morning, and was waiting for Judith and Peter when they returned from their weekend in Surrey on Sunday night.

Peter had told me this when he had brought me in the car from Fenbridge hospital early this morning. I had been there four days, ever since Max had taken me there on Friday night – or rather, in the small hours of Saturday morning.

I remembered very little about what had happened after I had been pulled out of the quarry. I had a vague recollection of lights and voices, and a rough car journey, and then being wheeled on a trolley into the Casualty department I had left so short a time before. I could just remember seeing David's anxious face peering down at me as I lay there, before drifting off into a shallow exhausted doze, could just remember seeing Max, too, as he leaned over me and whispered "good night" after I had been put to bed in the private wing of the hospital.

I hadn't seen him since, for as Peter had explained, he had been with the police, searching endlessly for Higgins who had again disappeared. His wife said she knew nothing more about him, although it had been she who had warned Max that her husband was in the area still, and had told him where he had been hiding. She knew her husband was still insanely convinced that I was the cause of all his troubles, knew he couldn't be trusted, and had decided to tell Max about the fact that he had reappeared.

"Which was just as well," Peter told me, as he drove carefully through the bright sunshiny roads back to Tetherdown after solicitously tucking me into the front seat with a blanket – which I protested I didn't need – around my knees. "If Max hadn't phoned Langham's Farm to see why you hadn't returned by one in the morning, I suppose you'd be in the quarry yet. But knowing where Higgins had been hiding, and seeing your car abandoned on the road, he realized you must be around, and went looking for you – "

He looked sideways at me, and then returned his attention to the road, and said with a heavily casual voice that didn't deceive me for a moment, "He was frantic – I've never seen a man in such a state as he was when we got back Sunday night. They still didn't know then how you were going to come through. And he was sick with worry for you. I'd say that he was – very deeply involved with you indeed."

I blushed hotly, and Peter looked at me again and chuckled.

"You too, hmm? I'm delighted. If anyone can get Max over the past and the stupid prejudices it left him with, it's you."

I looked at him curiously, "What past?"

"You don't know? He never told you?"

"He – he's never told me anything about himself. We've never talked at all, really. Apart from discussing thunderstorms – " and my lips curved as I remembered that strange evening.

"Well, it's gossip, in a way – "

"Not really, it might help. You see, we both – well – misunderstood each other," I said with painful honesty. "I thought he hated me – "

Peter laughed. "Did you? Very unperceptive of you. I spotted what was happening between you two weeks ago, even if you didn't realize it yourselves. All right, I'll tell you. It might – help to smooth the way for you both."

He stopped talking for a while, and concentrated on a tricky curve, and then started to talk again, not looking at me.

"Max was married before – to a girl he'd been at University with. He was very much in love with her, I think. Anyway, when they'd both qualified, he decided to go in for general practice, which he adores, because although he could have had a brilliant career as a specialist, he wanted to practise real medicine. Anyway, she pretended to agree with him, and they worked together for a while – "

"Yes?" I prompted, for he'd stopped.

"Well, she deceived him," Peter said awkwardly. "Just ran off one morning, to go and live with a consultant skin man they'd known in their student days, and left Max in the lurch."

"A skin man – a dermatologist. No wonder he was so scornful of Charles," I said, almost to myself.

"It didn't help," Peter said dryly. "He didn't talk about it – Max rarely talks to anyone – but I knew how he felt. Anyway, eventually he divorced her, and he's been living the life of a – a dedicated hermit ever since. Not good. Not good at all. If you can get him out of it, back into normal living again, it will be a wonderful thing for him – "

"And for me," I murmured, but so softly that Peter didn't hear me.

For I knew now. As I sat there in the warm sunshine watching Judith and her baby, I knew what I had been trying to hide from myself for some weeks now. I loved Max Lester very much indeed, more than I could have imagined I'd ever love anyone. The way I'd felt about Charles had paled into the weak thing which was all it had ever been

– a schoolgirlish infatuation. I knew now how Jeremy had felt for me – and knew too how easy it had been for him to get over it.

It was odd, to sit there waiting for Max to come back, waiting to see him again. I knew now that however long it would be before he arrived, however little he had to say, our relationship was a real and deep one. There was none of the sick frightened anticipation that had been part of the way I'd felt about Charles. There was just a deep sense of peace, a feeling of having come home at last, of having someone else to shoulder my burdens, someone else's burdens to carry. For that was what love was all about. Whatever happened to David and Fiona, now I had Max to help me. Whatever Max had suffered in the past, now he had me to help him. Peace.

There was a sound behind me, and I turned my head and saw him standing there, looking at me.

"Hello", I said softly, and smiled at him, letting all my feelings show in my too-expressive face.

"Hello yourself," he said and came and sat beside me, and took my bandaged hands gently in his and sat and looked at me.

"Did you find him?" I asked after a long pause.

He nodded. "Yes. Nothing more to fret about now. He's in hospital again – and this time they'll take good care of him."

"Good," I said, and turned my head and smiled at him again.

He leaned forwards and very gently kissed me, and I let my lips brush his, and knew really and finally that I had found the end of my road.

And then we turned, and sat together watching Judith playing with a fat baby on a rug under a copper beech tree on a hot summer morning in August. There was all the time in the world for talking, and planning, and exploring each other's minds and hearts and needs. Right now, we were just happy to be together, sitting in the garden of Downlands, our whole lives spread before us, our whole future in each other's hands.

The two of us. Together.